"So what do you

"You, Kelly. And She...

Even though she'd expected this, at least somewhat, she flinched but didn't stop walking.

"Who's that?" she asked. Part of her training when provided a new identity was to admit nothing, so she wasn't about to tell Alan she recognized that name. Her real name.

"That's good," he said. "You're at least complying with some of the instructions you were given. But you shouldn't have come here. That was completely against what you were told."

"Oh, really?" She kept her tone light. "I don't know what you're talking about."

The hand holding hers moved enough to swing her around, and suddenly Alan was looking down at her. Kelly could still see the anger on her companion's face, and it made her wince.

"I..." Before she could figure out how to finish, his mouth came down on hers.

His kiss was startlingly sexy, and so was the way his body soon molded to hers.

Get away from him, something inside her screamed. She could be in danger.

* * *

Dear Reader,

This is my second book about the ID Division of the US Marshals Service. The first was *Covert Attraction* (12/13).

I created the ID Division for the situation where a person knows about a crime that affects her but didn't witness it and can't provide other evidence against the guilty party. And then the guilty party threatens that person, but remains subtle about it.

In that case, the endangered person can't get into a witness protection program, since she can't testify in court or provide other evidence to help convict the guilty party. But she still needs help. And the guilty party still needs to be prosecuted.

That's where my ID Division comes in. It both helps create a new identity for the person in trouble, and also sends a team member undercover to locate the missing evidence to convict that guilty party.

And once again, in *Covert Alliance*, the woman whose identity was changed and the undercover operative looking for that evidence clash—yet find their mutual attraction irresistible.

I hope you enjoy *Covert Alliance*. Please come visit me at my website, lindaojohnston.com, and at my weekly blog, killerhobbies.blogspot.com. And yes, I'm on Facebook, too.

Linda O. Johnston

COVERT ALLIANCE

Linda O. Johnston

Withdrawn/ABCL

HARLEQUIN® ROMANTIC SUSPENSE

Recycling programs
for this product may
not exist in your area.

ISBN-13: 978-0-373-28147-3

Covert Alliance

Printed in U.S.A.

Linda O. Johnston loves to write. While honing her writing skills, she worked in advertising and public relations, then became a lawyer...and enjoyed writing contracts. Linda's first published fiction appeared in *Ellery Queen's Mystery Magazine* and won a Robert L. Fish Memorial Award for Best First Mystery Short Story of the Year. Linda now spends most of her time creating memorable tales of paranormal romance, romantic suspense and mystery. Visit her on the web at www.lindaojohnston.com.

As with *Covert Attraction*, *Covert Alliance* is dedicated to those in danger, and those in love.

And yes, as always, I dedicate this book to my wonderful husband, Fred.

Chapter 1

"Yes, I'll be glad to bring you—" Kelly Ladd froze in the middle of her response to her customer's question. She had just glanced toward the restaurant's front door.

Stan Grodon stood in the crowd that was just entering.

Stan Grodon, the murderous SOB. The reason she had returned to Blue Haven, California—as well as the reason she'd previously been forced to flee for her life. And now—

"Miss? Miss? I'd really like sausage instead of bacon in my three-cheese omelet. Is that okay?"

Kelly's attention returned quickly to the glare of the middle-aged lady in a too-tight Blue Haven Bulldogs T-shirt who sat with a couple of other similarly clad women at the round table nearest her. She stood between two of them, leaning slightly forward, a pad of paper and a pen in her hand to jot down their orders.

"I'm terribly sorry," she said soothingly, glad her voice wasn't cracking. "Of course you can have sausage instead of bacon. Are the types of cheese okay?"

Kelly forced herself to concentrate on taking the orders of all the women at the table, not watching the entrance of the city council members and others with them. Or at least not doing so overtly. She stood sideways so she wouldn't be too obvious.

But she did manage to observe them as they waited to be seated. Especially the man who had gotten away—so far—with killing his wife. Who had attempted to kill Kelly.

And who was now endangering his own son.

When Kelly headed to the next customer at the table, she allowed herself to turn just a little, to grab a quick look at the group. She had known that a few Blue Haven City Council members and some staff were expected here for a 9:00 a.m. breakfast. They'd sent someone ahead to make sure tables would be ready for them.

Which had also given Kelly time to prepare herself mentally—as much as she could—assuming Stan might be among them. And maybe the other man she anticipated, his aide, Paul Tirths.

Paul was not here, but Stan was. Kelly had played out this moment hundreds of times in her mind. Thousands. Yet she knew reality was unlikely to unfold exactly as she'd imagined.

She just hoped it soon allowed her, at last, to achieve her goals. And stay alive.

She forced herself to smile and act as if she was paying complete attention to what the next customer said. In fact, she was paying some attention. She had to. She was a waitress here, which included taking orders, serving and more. That was the cover she had created for herself. A perfect cover, since she had been fully aware of how popular this family-style café was with the local city council.

Plus, she now knew how to be the ultimate server, thanks to her new identity—although she'd unfortunately had to walk out on the job she had been given to start her new life.

And in doing so, she had undoubtedly incurred a lot of wrath that she would ultimately have to face.

But not yet. Now it was almost time. Time to see if her new looks, that new identity, her new persona, had all been changed sufficiently to make sure Stan couldn't recognize that she was actually Shereen Alsop, sister to Andi Grodon, the woman who'd been his wife.

The woman he had murdered just over a year ago. Whose body was never found.

"Thanks," Kelly finally said, smiling brightly at her customers. "I'll be back with your food soon."

She barely noticed their startled looks. Had they finished telling her what they wanted? No matter. She couldn't just stay there. Not now.

Along with the rest of his crowd, Stan now moved toward her as they followed the hostess. He was dressed nattily in an expensive-looking suit and was smiling, damn him, as he chatted with his fellow council members and others like he had nothing in the world on his conscience.

Kelly ached to confront him. Smash that smile right off his ugly, falsely charming face.

But not here. Not now. Not without answers—or Eli. She'd taken on a different identity on social media, too, and the scared recent posts from her nephew were the primary reason she had returned so impulsively.

If there had been any way of helping Eli remotely, she would have done it. She had tried to think of some way to do that so she wouldn't have to put herself in danger once more.

But she hadn't been able to just sit back and watch Eli's terror grow.

"They're here." Ella Berdeen, the restaurant's co-owner and manager, had joined Kelly near the row of tables that she had, at Ella's instruction, helped to set up. That had involved obtaining more information about timing and numbers from the guy who had requested the rearrangement, then getting enough patrons to move to different tables in the busy restaurant to provide space for the city council.

It had taken a little bribery, some drinks and pastries that were on the house, but it had all worked out in the end.

"I'll go tell the other servers," Kelly said hurriedly, feeling like a coward. But she didn't want to just stand there. And she would simply help to serve the food. She wouldn't take orders. The waitresses were more noticeable than the ones who simply brought the food out and set it quickly down in front of the patrons—perhaps having an opportunity to eavesdrop a little on what they said.

Even so, she wished her waitress uniform weren't so skimpy—a short black skirt beneath a snug and sleeveless white blouse. She knew Stan was a womanizer, and if he looked at her now, she wouldn't necessarily be able to tell if he was undressing her in his mind—or recognizing her.

"No, I'll tell them, and give me the orders you just wrote down. You start taking the orders of the council members and their staff. We have to accommodate their schedule." Ella's expression appeared irritated. In the few days since Kelly had started working here, she'd observed that despite what she made female servers wear, Ella liked to wear chic dresses over comfortable shoes, as she did now. Her hair was short and blond, and her smile never-ending—at least with her customers.

With her employees, like Kelly, she didn't try to hide it if she felt annoyed. Like now.

"Okay," Kelly said. But it wasn't okay. Her first protective measure was now decimated.

On the other hand, maybe it would be better if she knew right away if all the changes that had been made to her, via cosmetic surgery, dyed and restyled hair, lessons in makeup and comportment and posture, voice and more, had changed her appearance enough.

She would soon find out.

Kelly started to turn toward the table when she saw the man in a suit who'd been in here before. He had returned—the guy who had come to make sure things could be set up for this group quickly and who had answered her questions about the arrangement.

Not surprising. He would want to make sure that all was ready, as promised.

But that might not be all he was doing here. And that worried Kelly.

At first she'd thought him an aide to the council members. But as he'd continued to ask questions as well as answer them, she had begun to wonder if he was with the private security company hired to protect the council.

She—no, her alter ego, Shereen Alsop—had had some familiarity with Blue Haven Security and with its staff...then. Before she had fled the town of Blue Haven to avoid the threats to her life that she knew, but could not prove, had come from Stan.

Ella had called this man Alan. He had just reentered the restaurant behind the group, but now he slid in front, approaching Kelly. She wanted to flee into the kitchen. Instead, she stood her ground.

The last thing she wanted was to do anything that might make her conspicuous, especially now, with Stan in the room.

Besides, her suspicion of this guy could just be a self-protective instinct. She couldn't trust anyone. She didn't dare.

"Good job getting this set up, Kelly," Alan said to her immediately. Ella had told him her name earlier, too.

A feeling of warmth passed through her—unwanted heat. Sure, he was attractive. Sexy.

But she didn't dare even hint at flirting with him.

"Thanks," she said, making sure she did everything possible to stay within her role.

Alan was over six feet tall. His deep brown eyes regarded her from beneath craggy dark brows that matched his short hair, and he smiled.

But something in his expression made Kelly think he was trying to keep up appearances, too. Maybe because she suspected everyone these days.

Or maybe because she actually knew who this guy was.

"Hey, can we place our orders now?" someone called from beside her. "We're in a hurry."

Kelly needed to move away from Alan, and so she

turned to respond. But she knew that voice. It was Stan's.

Which would be less risky—staying here and talking with this possible security guy who might have a different agenda from the rest of his team?

Or confronting Stan for the first time?

"Go ahead," Ella said from her other side, and the choice was taken from her.

When she glanced in Alan's direction, she saw him nod slightly, with a small grin on his rugged, amused face that suggested he understood her dilemma.

Was she just reading into his appearance, his actions, because she suspected there would be someone in this town who was also undercover, but officially so?

Well, this wasn't the time to worry about it. Right now, she needed to confront Stan. Sort of. While staying in character, and praying that her new appearance worked, and Stan didn't recognize her.

And thus she would at last be able to accomplish what had become her life's mission: protecting Eli and finally getting the evidence on Stan.

Alan Correy watched the gorgeous waitress who turned toward the tables of city council members.

The woman he had never met, yet already knew.

When he had come in before as a staff member of Blue Haven Security—his job here, while undercover—to request the tables, Ella had said her name was Kelly. And Alan had previously been instructed to keep an eye out for the woman now known as Kelly Ladd. He had been sent her photo as she'd looked originally, along with the last time they'd seen her, by his boss over his secure phone connection. Was this her?

Maybe.

That woman had taken full advantage of his real employer, the ID Division of the US Marshals Service. They had provided her protection as well as an identity change. But she left the job she had been given in her new life, disappeared without permission from the division's head, Judge Treena Avalon, or anyone else.

She had been expected to show up here. Apparently she had.

This Kelly resembled the photo, although her hair was softer, curlier and a darker brown, pulled away from her face with a narrow band. Her cheekbones were more prominent, her lips narrower. Her face could have won beauty contests.

But the real Kelly, in addition to having had her looks modified, would also have been instructed in ways to further disguise herself if necessary.

Instead of immediately rushing over to the tables to take orders, Kelly continued looking at Alan for an instant. He had a sense that she was assessing him the way he was assessing her. That she suspected who he was, too.

But then she quickly pulled a pad from the pocket of her skimpy skirt and approached the table.

The person nearest to her, who'd just commanded her attention, was the reason Alan was here in Blue Haven.

And if he was right about who she was, Stan Grodon might in fact be the reason this attractive waitress was here, too. For similar reasons to his.

If so, she was endangering everything Alan stood for. Endangering herself—again—as well.

He would need to stop her. Oh, yeah.

But for now, he would ignore his deep-seated irritation—and her sexiness—and simply observe.

Could she do this?

She had to. Eli's well-being was at stake.

Kelly quickly turned her back on the man who sent sparks of nervousness up her spine, whom she believed could ruin everything here for her—and for Eli.

But if she tried, she could ruin everything for him, too. Not that she wanted to.

The tables, all pushed together, seated four on each side and two along the end. A small bouquet of pink roses decorated the middle. The council group members were chatting amiably, although Kelly caught occasional brief eye rolls from some of them.

"Hello," she said with a huge, contrived smile as she planted herself between Stan and another council member, one who looked familiar but whom she didn't place. "What can I bring you gentlemen?"

"A tall mug of your strongest and best coffee," said the short, older man.

"Me, too," said Stan. "Get yourself one, as well. Then you can sit on my lap and drink it."

It was all Kelly could do to prevent herself from gagging. Or, more preferable, grabbing the pitcher of water from the table and bashing Stan in the head with it.

His face was round, his hair thinning, his wide grin evil and unsexy, but he undoubtedly still considered himself the world's greatest gift to women.

For now, Kelly had to go along with it. "Well, thank you, sir," she said in the new soft and lower voice in which she'd been coached. "But I'm sure you'll understand that I have to help your friends get their meals, too."

She did it. She looked straight into his eyes and all but batted her lashes.

If he was going to recognize her, better that it happen now, with all these people around, than later.

"Oh, I understand, all right," he responded, giving her a huge and ugly wink. "But I come here often. We'll grab coffee—and more—another time. You're new at the Haven, aren't you?"

"Yes, sir." She made herself pause. "It's such a wonderful place. Filled with wonderful people." She didn't glance away, despite how painful it was to watch him.

Did he know who she was?

Apparently not. A brief feeling of relief shot through her as he continued to treat her like a total stranger. A total *female* stranger he chose to flirt with.

"Sure is," he said. "Like the rest of our Blue Haven. Welcome, and I hope you stay a long, long time. I'm Stan, by the way."

"Me, too, sir," she lied. "And I'm Kelly."

She forced herself to continue to take his order— ham and eggs and all the makings of a big breakfast. The others also gave their orders, although a couple of additional waitstaff now joined Kelly to help.

When she was finally finished, she saw that Alan, the good-looking guy she didn't dare trust, had seated himself with another man in a suit at a smaller table nearby.

He was watching her. And as she hurried into the kitchen to place the orders, she turned back. Alan's gaze hadn't left her. As sexy as she considered the man, she felt certain that physical attraction was far from his motive for observing her.

Alan might be the person who was supposed to be here, undercover, to bring Stan down.

But at the same time he might bring Kelly down, too.

Chapter 2

Kelly wished she could stand there and eavesdrop on Stan's conversations—unobtrusively, without encouraging his disgusting flirtation with her. But she knew she had to stay on top of the requests made by all customers at the tables to which she'd been assigned. At least that included the one where Stan sat.

She didn't believe he would spill the information she sought right here, in public. But he might drop even just a tiny hint that could lead her, eventually, to what she needed.

Consequently, she passed the table often, refilling water glasses and coffee cups, smiling and inquiring whether everything was okay. Stan had started a loud, friendly conversation with one of his colleagues and more or less ignored her, except to ask for a coffee refill now and then. Kelly also made sure that Alan, as well as his tablemate, were satisfied with the service. To them, she was a server here, and that was all.

She hoped.

Kelly didn't realize how much of a strain it all was until the entire group, presumed security guys included, finally filed out of the restaurant. Only then did she start breathing normally again.

"Good job," Ella told the entire group of servers as they stood in the kitchen awaiting the next food items to bring out to remaining and new customers.

"She always says that," Tobi Marolo whispered out of the corner of her mouth. Tobi had told Kelly she had worked there for decades, even though she was only in her late twenties, around Kelly's age. When Kelly gently called her on it, she admitted it only felt like she'd practically been born working at this place. "It's supposed to make us feel happy and actually do a good job…next time," Tobi continued.

Kelly laughed. She really did feel happy—or at least relieved. Her second hurdle since arriving back in Blue Haven had been leaped, and seemed to have been successful. The first had been landing this job. The second was seeing Stan in person and not being identified by him. He'd never have simply ignored her if he'd thought she could possibly be Shereen—or anyone else who mattered to him.

She still had no idea how she would accomplish hurdle number three: seeing her nephew, Eli, the real reason she had broken promises and rules when her identity had been changed for her protection, and she'd returned to Blue Haven.

Hurdle number four? She had anticipated she might face it—having to deal with someone undercover here who was part of the Identity Division, the government agency that had helped her tremendously but whose commands she was now ignoring. She just hadn't thought she'd have to face it this soon. If Alan was who she believed he was, that obstacle was now potentially as urgent as the others.

And then there was the most critical, number five: finding a way, at last, to bring Stan down and help Eli.

For the rest of the morning, Kelly went through the usual rituals of greeting customers, handing them menus, making suggestions and taking their orders. Then she served them with a smile, making sure their experiences here were completely positive.

She didn't always love the aromas floating through the kitchen, particularly the occasional burning of a dish. And it was tiring to be on her feet all the time. Plus, trays full of food could be quite heavy.

Then there was the uniform she wore. Stan wasn't the only one who eyed her as if she were bed-bait. Maybe that had been Alan's only interest in her, too, despite her suspicions. If he weren't security in any form, she might even have considered reciprocating, since the guy was pretty darned hot.

But many men seemed to notice her here—and not only her. Ella had chosen the cutesy outfits for the female servers who made up most of the waitstaff, Kelly was sure, to appeal to male customers. The Haven was essentially a glorified coffee shop, but it had a longtime reputation for catering to the powers-that-be in Blue Haven. It didn't hurt to give the men some eye candy while they were here.

Or that was what Kelly had heard, anyway.

Soon, the early lunch crowd began to arrive. Kelly

ramped up her energy and her serving skills, but was disappointed when she didn't see anyone she recognized as being on the city council. She glanced outside as often as she could, toward the other restaurants and shops across the street and foot traffic coming from the east, the direction of the city offices.

But nothing and no one useful to her appeared.

Until...

When it was nearly noon and the kitchen was crowded with servers entering with trays of empty plates and leaving again with food to serve, Ella appeared from the office near the restrooms at the back. "We need a few of you for something different this afternoon," she said. "The city council members who were here enjoyed their breakfast, as usual. They've now called a special session for all the council members. I'm glad to say they've ordered in a buffet-style lunch at their offices. Twice in one day! And we won't let them down. Who's willing to go over there and deliver and set up the food?"

Kelly almost cheered in her delight. That was exactly why she had applied for a job at this restaurant. But she caught herself and forced a slight smile that she hoped appeared more as if she wanted to please her boss than anything else. "I'll be glad to, Ella." Glad? Heck, she'd be thrilled.

And she really was thrilled when Ella chose her, among several of the waitstaff who also volunteered.

Alan looked forward to a busy afternoon—one in which he could actually get some work done. Work that he was really here to do.

After he briefly visited the moderate-sized computer

room that the Blue Haven Police Department allowed the private security force to use as an outpost in the main government building, an ad hoc meeting of the entire city council was called. They were to discuss some vital matters about street widenings—vital to the town, but not of particular interest to Alan.

Yes, he'd have to do his best to ensure that the city council members remained safe. But that didn't mean he had to sit in on every session. Popping in and out while looking as if he were patrolling the building and surrounding area would be enough.

Too bad he hadn't known this morning, while still at the Haven, that he'd remain on duty with no break. He could have bought his lunch to go. Taken an opportunity to speak with that server Kelly once more. Maybe even confirmed she was who he figured she was.

Plus, spending a little additional time with her would provide a bit of pleasure as well as an opportunity for professional observation.

He shrugged off that thought. He'd see her again sometime. Soon, in fact. He would plan for it. But he had to make sure he didn't keep her on his mind. He had other things to think about.

Like doing both his jobs.

For now, Alan was alone in the security headquarters room. He typed his password into the computer and saw the views on a half dozen security cameras.

Everything looked fine, at least for now.

The city council offices were located in the Blue Haven Government Plaza. The plaza was about ten years old, new enough to have been built in a higher-security age. There was a screening system for the public at the entrance, plus security cameras on all floors.

That should have made Alan's job easier—and perhaps it would if he were merely part of the Blue Haven City Council's private security force. But it made it harder for him to get away on his own to conduct the investigation he was really here to do.

He'd managed once, though, to sneak into Stan Grodon's office early on when he'd first arrived in town and gotten on his computer. Surprise, surprise—there had been no open files containing anything about his missing wife. Even the encrypted files appeared to be about finances, not Andi Grodon.

He had to approach his investigation in other ways.

At least the council members treated the security force just like their own staff, acting friendly to them and even asking them to do things beyond their actual responsibilities—such as getting the breakfast set up, as Alan had done earlier. He could act friendlier to them that way—and hopefully learn more. In fact, he was milking that aspect of his cover job.

But right now, it was time to get busy.

As he left the room, Dodd Frankler, a senior member of the security detail, was just entering. He'd joined Alan earlier at the Haven, and now, along with his usual dark suit, he wore his typically wary expression. "Hey, did you hear that the council's meeting in half an hour?" Dodd asked.

Alan nodded. "I was just on my way to the council chamber to check it out ahead of time."

"They're eating lunch there, too. A delivery order's already been sent over to the Haven. You'd think that after having breakfast there this morning, they'd be tired of that place's food."

"You know it's pretty good stuff," Alan countered.

"And their selections include something for everyone."
He didn't like the way his face automatically started
tightening into a wry grin as he thought of what else
was at the Haven besides good food. But the restaurant
was well staffed, so that new server Kelly was unlikely
to be coming here with the food.

Even if she did, who said the security staff would
even get to look at the lunch, let alone eat any? They'd
have patrols to perform outside the meeting area. A bit
of overkill for such a small town, Alan thought, but it
worked well for what he needed to accomplish.

He hurried down the wide, well-lit hallway, along
with a fair number of government workers he recognized, including members of the mayor's staff, plus
some visitors he didn't know. As always, he stayed
alert, watching for signs that anyone had an agenda
besides using the halls for getting to the offices they
sought. People were mostly in groups, chattering.

He noticed a couple of school-age guys heading up
the stairway. They'd been around before, usually later
in the day, but Alan knew that a new program was just
starting locally where kids could pop in during their
study hall times and earn credit for learning about city
government by volunteering for small activities that
would help their council members. Some were chil-
dren of those who worked for the city.

One of the two kids was Councilman Grodon's kid,
Eli. The other was Councilwoman Arviss's son, Cal.
Maybe Alan could go cheer them on later…and perhaps learn something of value this time, though he'd
talked with them a time or two before. Alan followed
them upstairs.

The boys walked to the fourth floor. It was where

Alan would have gone anyway since the council chamber was there. Along the hall on the way were council members' offices, assigned by their seniority. The mayor's office was one floor above them.

The boys remained ahead of Alan. As he'd anticipated, they entered Susan Arviss's office. He would look for them there later.

As he continued down the hall, he glanced at the names in glass-enclosed sign holders on the walls. Grodon's was close to the end. He was one of the longest-sitting members of the council, although he wasn't the president. That was Councilwoman Regina Joralli's position.

Alan soon reached the large meeting room and stepped inside. The room held a huge table in the center, surrounded by wooden chairs made to resemble small, upholstered thrones. A bunch of staff members were already there, chatting together and making sure the chairs were in the right places and the table was clean. Joralli's primary assistant was also there, placing handouts at each seat, probably on the matter they were to meet about.

Everything looked secure enough, but he and the others on that detail would keep checking.

And while the meeting occurred, he might have an opportunity to do some further checking into the undercover assignment that had brought him here by having a friendly chat with those boys. He had been around long enough to start being recognized by the locals, so it was time to start pushing further into what he had really come for.

Dodd joined him as he walked around the room. "Couple of the other guys are downstairs now," he said.

"Hancock told me to come up here and look around." Nevil Hancock, their boss.

They remained there for another ten minutes, watching who entered and left the room, and checking the hallway, too.

This part of the job could get monotonous, but that was a good thing—no security breaches or other issues to worry about.

The council members began entering. Alan and Dodd remained until they all were seated. Then back into the hall to keep their eyes open for anyone who shouldn't be attempting to go into council chambers.

Alan preceded Dodd toward the door—and stopped.

Approaching were several familiar-looking people carrying large plastic bags that were undoubtedly filled with food from the Haven.

And one of them was that sexy server Kelly.

Kelly shouldn't have felt surprised to see Alan near the room where the city council was meeting when she approached with the other restaurant staff members. She had suspected that he and the other man were at the restaurant earlier at least ostensibly to protect some council members, so it was natural for them to be here now doing the same.

Just like it was natural for her, these days, to observe people and what they were doing.

Alan and his colleague had just exited the room Kelly, Ella and Tobi were heading for. They stood outside the door. The man's eyes seemed to focus directly on her.

If he was going to watch her, she should at least act friendly toward him, no matter how she felt. Maybe she could even render him off guard, although she suspected that any undercover member of the ID Division, if that's what he was, would never be off guard.

As the other servers walked by the men into the room, Kelly smiled a little. "Hi, guys. Fancy seeing you again." She looked directly at the one who'd especially attracted her attention. "Hey, are you following the council members to protect them?"

The expression on his handsome face grew quizzical. "Why do you ask?"

She knew she was right about that, at least, since he had answered her question with a question. "Because I'm curious," she said. "And I suspect you are, too." But why was she teasing him? It might be a big mistake to even talk to him anymore. "Sorry. I just guessed you're in security, and I admire that."

"Maybe we should hire you," Alan said. "You do seem pretty alert. What do you think, Dodd?"

The other man—Dodd, apparently—looked a lot older than Alan, and Kelly suspected he'd been doing security work for a long time. He didn't smile. In fact, he didn't look at all happy about the conversation. "I think we need to check the hallway, then come back here."

"Fine." Alan nodded briefly at her as if in goodbye, and both men started walking toward the elevators from which Kelly and the others had come.

Kelly entered the room. It was large, and the main center of focus was a huge rectangular table in the middle, where the city council members all sat. Kelly recognized the few who'd patronized the Haven for breakfast. Even those she hadn't seen before were dressed in suits.

Among them, unsurprisingly, was Stan. He sat at the far side of the table, his black suit jacket on, his round face smirking beneath his thinning brown hair. He faced the door where Kelly had just entered, chatting with the man on his left as if he hadn't a care in the world.

And Kelly wanted to shake him. Or do something worse.

The woman who sat at the end of the table was Councilwoman Regina Joralli. She'd been in politics for a while, and Kelly recognized her from when she had lived there in her previous life. Stan was right beside her.

Kelly knew he had aspirations to replace Regina as council president. Or at least he had before. He was so egotistical that Kelly figured the only way that might have changed was if he decided to run for mayor.

Unless, of course, he was concentrating only on raking in bribe money—and hiding her sister's murder while abusing their son. But with an ego like his, Kelly figured he still wanted it all.

Despite the fact that every seat around the table was filled, it was still twenty minutes before the time Kelly had been told that the session was officially scheduled to begin. Lunch apparently came first. The room was abuzz with conversation as Kelly joined her colleagues from the restaurant and helped to lay out the food on a compact table at the end of the room, turning it into a buffet. She assisted in making it look decorative yet practical, where the council members could pick up tasty sandwiches, small salads and cookies, as well as soft drinks.

"I think we're all set here," Ella eventually told Regina Joralli. "Anything else you need?"

"It all looks good," the council president said. "Thanks."

That was their cue to leave, Kelly knew. Which was fine. She remained invisible here to Stan as one among many lowly servers he could flirt with, but being inside this room any longer wouldn't get her any of the information she sought.

She followed the others out the door. They all turned left toward the elevators.

Kelly didn't want to leave the building just yet, though. Instead, she glanced at the placards of each council member's name on the wall near the offices. She knew she couldn't just drop into Stan Grodon's and find whatever she needed—particularly since she knew that security was present on this floor, although she didn't see Alan or his buddy Dodd just then. She did, however, see a few cameras mounted near the tops of the walls.

Even so, she could get the lay of the land.

"Excuse me, Ella," she said, hurrying to catch up with her boss. "I'm going to find the restroom here. I'll be back at the restaurant soon."

Ella's cool eyes scanned her. "You feeling okay?"

Obviously she'd send Kelly home if she was sick with anything she could pass along.

"Fine." Kelly smiled what she hoped was an embarrassed smile. "I just drank a little too much coffee this morning."

"Okay. Fine. See you later." They'd reached the elevators, and the door to one opened as soon as Ella pressed the button—an indication of the woman's lot in life, Kelly figured. Everything seemed to work out well for her.

Well, it would for Kelly, too—as soon as she was able to find her nephew and help him. He'd be in classes now, and she didn't want to appear obvious by hanging around his school. She had to figure out a good way to see him. Talk to him.

But while she figured that out, she also wanted to devise a plan to get the right evidence against Stan. No one, not even her thug of a brother-in-law, would suspect that was what Kelly Ladd was up to—unlike Shereen Alsop.

Well, there was one possible exception to that: Alan.

For now, she figured she had better do as she'd told Ella and start at the restroom before conducting any further exploration of this floor. When she came out, she could scout to see who else was around. She had been here before, when she'd been Shereen, and had accompanied Andi on scheduled visits now and then, sometimes even to see Stan. But more than a year had passed. The council members could be in different offices now.

Maybe she could become close friends with someone who worked here—someone who could get her into Stan's.

But what she'd done before hadn't gotten her anything useful. And neither would being in here.

Instead, she was feeling rather desperate to plan her next move: figure out how to see Eli and check in person how he was doing…and get him out of here if all was as bad as she thought, assuming his posts on social media reflected his reality.

She had come up with that other identity there so she

could at least watch him remotely, even if she couldn't communicate with him. His sorrow at his mother's disappearance, and then his aunt's, had been overtaken by his apparent desperation and fear. That was why she had come. It had been an impulse. It had been a necessity.

She nearly reached the restroom—and stopped. The men's room door had opened. Kelly thought she must be hallucinating.

Because the first person to walk through that door into the hallway was Alan.

And he was followed by her nephew, Eli.

Chapter 3

Kelly wanted to laugh. She wanted to cry. Mostly, she wanted to dash over and throw her arms around her nephew.

No, Shereen's nephew. That's what she had to remember.

Realizing that she had stopped walking, she started forward again. Another boy exited the men's room and caught up with Eli. He bent his head toward Eli, who was about the same height, maybe five feet, and the two of them laughed. They passed her, and Eli, busy talking to his friend, didn't even look at her.

That was a good thing. Not that he was likely to recognize her, with the way her appearance had been changed—including her posture, gestures and nearly everything about her. Externally, at least.

The hardest part was that she forced herself not to

look at him any longer, except for allowing herself to glance at him peripherally down the hall while she strolled by.

Was that a bruise on his cheek? She wanted so much to turn and stare at his sweet young face and check it out.

But she couldn't. Not here, and not now.

"Hi, Kelly." It was Alan, and his voice startled her. He had stopped walking and let the kids pass by him.

"Er, hi." She cocked her head a little and forced herself to send him a flirtatious grin. "Keeping an eye on things everywhere, aren't you? I'm just hitting the ladies' room before I head back to the restaurant." She hurried past him and entered the restroom.

Fortunately it was empty, since she was suddenly breathing hard, her eyes closed, her mind swirling.

She had bumped into hurdle number three without anticipating or planning for it. She had seen Eli. But where could she go from here?

She needed to talk to him. Find out what was really going on with him. Was his father abusing him, as he'd hinted on that social media site? She was sure it had to be true. Eli had always been such a straightforward child.

And that red spot on his face. Was that proof, or her imagination, or just a harmless bruise that kids sometimes got when roughhousing with friends?

She knew where he lived, of course—assuming they hadn't moved. Even so, he must live with his father. With Stan. And that meant Kelly couldn't just walk up to their door, ring the bell and invite herself in for a chat.

He was thirteen years old now. She knew he still

went to the same school, since Eli mentioned it on-line. But since she couldn't start stalking him there, ei-ther, she had decided to begin by observing Stan first, someplace where she wouldn't be particularly noticed. Someplace where a plan was sure to come to her.

Only now that she had seen not only Stan but Eli, too, she was stumped. And frustrated. And scared, and angry, and so many more emotions that she couldn't put names to.

She had been so close to her sister. Had loved Andi so much. She missed her terribly.

Andi had to be dead, or she would have been in touch. And Kelly's determination to save Eli was one way of demonstrating her love—and her despair at no longer having her sister around.

Kelly looked into the mirror above the sink, over her shoulder, as if her sister might suddenly appear there. "I'll take care of him now, Andi," she whispered aloud. "I promise."

The restroom door started to open. Kelly fled into one of the stalls and locked the door, then waited until she heard the other woman leave again before she flushed, washed her hands and exited the bathroom. By then, she had calmed herself a bit.

She had realized one thing, at least. Eli had been talking to Alan when she'd first noticed them. They seemed friendly enough with each other. Did they know each other, or were they just being cordial here, in the plaza?

She had to find that out. She also needed to learn why Eli was there, on an afternoon when his father wasn't available to meet with him because of the lunch-time council session.

As she walked slowly back down the hall, past the closed office doors, she heard nothing from the one with Stan's name on the wall plaque outside it. If Eli had come to visit or spend time in his dad's office, he was being quiet. Those were probably Stan's instructions to him. He'd never liked interruptions to his work, especially from his family.

From not only Eli, but his wife, Andi, too.

Kelly gritted her teeth but forced her thoughts off her missing—dead—sister. She was here for Eli.

A couple of offices down, she thought she heard a muffled voice. It was probably a secretary talking on the phone.

As she neared the far end of the hallway where the elevators were, she noticed that one door was ajar—Councilwoman Susan Arviss's office, according to the plaque on the outer wall. She was new, hadn't been a council member when Shereen had left town. Her office was one of the farthest from Council President Regina Joralli's.

Kelly heard giggles emanating from inside—like two young boys having a good time?

Would a total stranger, with no hidden agenda, peek inside while walking by? Maybe. She'd play it that way.

Or…no. She had a reason to peek inside. She'd already flirted a bit with Alan. He would be her excuse for checking out that office, even if he wasn't there. But he'd been chatting with Eli before, when they'd both come out of the men's room.

Suddenly, the bleak, bland government office hallway seemed to warm a bit.

Kelly stopped outside the partly open door and smiled slightly. It was a smile that she had practiced before, in front of mirrors, to ensure it looked different from Shereen's smile.

The two boys sat at the secretary's desk. Their attention seemed fully captured by what they were doing. It appeared that they were stuffing envelopes.

Kelly just watched for a moment. Then she saw a movement near her, to the side of the door. She startled, swallowed a gasp—then intentionally broadened her smile. It was Alan.

"Well, here you are." She tried to sound as if she'd been searching for him. "I wondered if I should call someone in security since this door was open."

"No need. I'm right here, and all's well."

"It certainly is."

Was that too much flirtation? At least it gave her a reason for being here. It wasn't difficult at all to continue looking at Alan that way. She still thought that, at another time, under other circumstances, she would have had fun flirting with a guy as hot as him.

Now, though, it was only a ruse. Too bad.

She noticed then that both boys had stopped what they were doing. She drew her gaze away from Alan's inquisitive brown eyes as if it were almost painful to do so and looked toward the desk.

"What have we here?" she asked in a friendly manner. "I don't think these young gentlemen are city council members, are they? Or maybe they're office staff, although if so, Councilwoman Arviss must have robbed schools to hire them."

Both boys laughed. "She's my mom," said the one Kelly hadn't met before. "She lets us do stuff here like get things ready to mail for her. We're like interns, and we get school credit for it."

"Wow," Kelly said. "Sounds like fun, and you get credit? Now I know why you're here."

She kept her eyes on the Arviss boy, not quite looking into Eli's face. He wasn't generally shy, but nor was he particularly outspoken. Still, she wished he would say something.

When he remained quiet, Kelly looked toward Alan. "And you? Do you get any credit for getting things ready to mail for the councilwoman?"

Both boys appeared to find that especially funny and laughed again, louder this time.

"I only gather points here that I hope to turn in someday to my credit if I somehow run afoul of city council," Alan said, his expression serious, but only for a moment. Then he smiled, too.

"So what kinds of things do you help the councilwoman mail?" Kelly's gaze returned first to Arviss's son, then turned briefly on to Eli.

"She says it fosters good relationships with her constituents to send them friendly snail mail letters sometimes that say what's going on in the city and what new stuff she's proposing while she's in office."

That was Eli! Kelly was thrilled. He sounded like her smart nephew, and it was again all she could do just to stand there and treat him like a young stranger.

Plus, her heart was pounding. Up close and personal like this, would he recognize her? Sure, she looked different. Sounded different. But still…

Fortunately, he just glanced at her without staring too hard.

"Very interesting," she said, relaxing just a little. She wanted to ask why Eli volunteered here and not for his father, although as Kelly, she wouldn't know that he, too, was a council member's son. Besides, she already knew the answer.

Maybe Councilwoman Arviss would encourage kids to come in and help her for school credit, but Councilman Stan Grodon would not—even if one of those kids happened to be his own son.

The kids just looked at her expectantly now, as if they assumed she'd say something else. But as much as she wanted to say—and do—now wasn't the time.

Reluctantly, she only said, "Well, have fun." She turned back toward Alan, who was still watching her. "You, too. Maybe I'll see you again at the restaurant sometime."

"I'm sure you will," he said, causing an unanticipated current of heat to flow through her, as if he were suggesting that they do a lot more than just say hi to each other if he came to the Haven to eat.

Kelly made herself leave then in a hurry, throwing a goodbye over her shoulder and waving.

She felt confused. And needy. She had to figure out a way to talk to Eli.

And to avoid talking too much to Alan.

Alan had an idea what that had been about. A good idea. He didn't like it. Although...

Oh, he was more than pleased to see Kelly again so soon. And to have her flirt with him again? Under other circumstances, if he weren't on duty, he'd not only have flirted back, but would have done his utmost to make sure they scheduled a date that night for dinner, drinks...and, if possible, a lot more.

But Alan's instincts were screaming out that he

needed to talk with her, ensure she didn't ruin things. And he always trusted his instincts.

Which was why he left Councilwoman Arviss's office briefly to watch Kelly sashay down the hall, still wearing that skimpy waitress's outfit. Oh, yeah, he enjoyed that view, with her appealing, compact behind flowing gently from side to side.

He saw the elevator door open, and she disappeared inside. Probably a good thing, he told himself. She was most likely going back to her restaurant and wouldn't cause any trouble, for now at least.

He returned to where the boys were stuffing those envelopes. He wasn't sure what their schedule was, but while talking with them briefly before, he'd figured that at least one of their study halls, when they could come here and do their volunteer work for credit, was around lunchtime on Thursdays. He had seen them last week at about the same time, and once in between.

He figured a little friendliness by a security staff member wouldn't look too out of place here by the folks in charge, especially since that was the way they were treated, too.

And eavesdropping on young Eli Grodon just might lead to some information he could follow up on for his real assignment—although it hadn't yet.

"Hey, Alan," Cal Arviss said when Alan was once more standing just inside the room. "Do you know when that big meeting will be over? We need to go back to school in a few minutes, and I want to say bye to my mom."

"Sorry," Alan responded. "I got the impression this one could be a long one. Want me to check?"

"Yes, please."

Alan left the two kids alone for a short while to go into the conference room. He entered the room cautiously, nodding toward Dodd, who had remained there to provide continuous security.

It appeared that the council members—and Dodd—were mostly still nibbling on their lunches and pontificating about how important the road widening under discussion could be to the town. Or not, since there were also opposing council members.

From what he gathered during his quick observation, it appeared that both Stan Grodon and Susan Arviss were in favor of approving the widening proposal, and Council President Joralli was against it for budget reasons.

Nothing indicated a quick end to the meeting. And Alan had no doubt that the kids would be unwelcome here.

He nodded again toward his colleague and left to report to the young men that their parents were still involved in their council session. Cal looked disappointed.

But Eli appeared relieved.

Alan walked them both down the hall, into the elevator, then out of the building. Other security staff members, as well as uniformed members of the Blue Haven PD, were on patrol outside the large plaza building, in the parking lot and around the busy street outside, and the school wasn't far away. Alan figured the kids would get back just fine.

Besides, the greatest threat to Eli, as far as Alan could tell, remained upstairs in the council meeting.

He needed to return there soon to coordinate with Dodd—but no one would pay attention to him if he took a short break now. He liked to check in with his real employer, the Covert Investigations Unit of the ID Division, as frequently as possible. He'd done so this morning, before reporting to work. He often contacted them in the middle of his workday to make sure there wasn't anything extra they wanted him to do while the city council members were most easily accessible.

After the two boys reached the next block, Alan strode down the wide stone steps, ignoring the other people coming and going. He slipped away from the plaza and around the corner into the parking lot shared by all Blue Haven government buildings. There, he got into the driver's seat of the car he was using here, a somewhat beat-up gray SUV, and locked the doors. Then he pulled his mobile phone from his pocket.

He had a text from his boss, Judge Treena Avalon. It was brief and to the point. He was to call her ASAP. It was important. She'd sent it about an hour ago.

Wasting no time, Alan pushed the button for the judge's cell phone. She answered almost immediately.

"Alan. Just checking in. Everything okay there?" Her voice was strong and intimidating. That was who Judge Treena was: demanding, no-nonsense, intense. But she was also kind, especially to the subjects taken on by the ID Division. She cared about both them and her staff.

"Fine," he said, "but no news yet."

"Then you haven't run into Kelly Ladd?"

Should he protect the woman he had met, who might be this Kelly, and after the same evidence he sought?

If he told Judge Treena he had not only seen her but talked to her several times, the judge might tell him to get her alone and order her back to the life the

ID Division had created for her, where she had promised to stay.

On the other hand, she might actually be an asset to him here, if they could work together—and if she helped him rather than hindered him.

That was his preference. The fact that she was one gorgeous woman he would have liked, under other circumstances, to get to know better was irrelevant.

It had to be.

If things changed and Kelly did get in his way, he could notify the judge that he had indeed located her.

But for now...

"Not as far as I know," he lied. "But I'm keeping my eyes open for her. And I'm hoping to gather some of that hard evidence we're looking for here soon."

Chapter 4

Kelly felt exhausted that afternoon. She realized it was probably more related to adrenaline and stress than actually having worked harder than she had previously in the few days since she had begun as a server here. But whatever the cause, she couldn't allow it to show now that she'd returned to the busy-as-usual restaurant. After seeing Eli, the last thing she wanted was to irritate Ella and jeopardize the job that was her cover.

The job that had let her get near and observe her nephew, and had the potential of allowing her continued access to him, at least sporadically. She hoped.

The job that got her into Stan's presence. Now she just had to figure out the best way she, as Kelly, could bring him down.

And she couldn't help worrying about Alan and his involvement with the city council—and more—and his potential interference. But she would figure out a way to deal with him.

She had to.

At least time seemed to move swiftly as she wove her way through the tables assigned to her for the rest of the day, the rear corner that managed to stay quite occupied despite being farthest from the door.

As she worked, she allowed her concentration to ebb just a little when she felt she could. Her mind kept analyzing what had happened earlier.

Yes, she had seen the one person she'd really hoped to: Eli. She had also seen Stan, and the fact that he, like Eli, hadn't recognized her was a really good thing.

But one person she'd been watching for hadn't appeared. She still hadn't seen Stan's assistant, Paul Tirths. Was Paul still around?

When Andi had disappeared and Kelly's alter ego, Shereen, had sought help and answers from anyone who knew Andi or her husband or both, Paul had been the one who'd hinted strongly that Stan had killed his wife and hidden her body. Later, he'd denied having said anything that could have led Kelly to draw such a heinous conclusion, especially about his boss—but she had believed he was lying then, not previously.

He had said nothing concrete. Nothing that could prove what had happened to Andi or lead to her body.

Then there had been the threats to Shereen for daring to question Stan's involvement in Andi's disappearance: speeding cars that nearly hit her while she was crossing city streets at night, even the street outside her apartment. No injury, fortunately, but only at times there were no witnesses, so no license plates, no vehicle identification. No perpetrator caught.

The last straw for Shereen was the night a bullet was fired through her bedroom window. No one witnessed the shooter, and although the type of gun was identified from the bullet, its owner wasn't.

Was that because local cops were protecting Stan?

And Shereen could provide no evidence to the authorities about Andi, or about the fact that she, too, was being targeted, except for that one bullet. All she could supply were claims…and questions.

So, ultimately, she had fled.

But now wasn't the time to focus on any of that. Kelly had to continue to do an excellent job as a restaurant server—and she would.

Some of her latest customers appeared to be women out for the afternoon, maybe enjoying time away from their kids in school. Another group of women were all clad in suits and dresses and appeared to be holding some kind of business meeting. A few guys in exercise outfits, possibly bicyclists, came in to take a break, and then there were several couples who could have been on midafternoon dates.

Speculating on who they were and their backgrounds helped to keep Kelly going. She attempted to recognize anyone, especially people who might recognize *her*. Fortunately, that didn't appear to be an issue.

Her fellow server Tobi got into her standard quips and observations about their customers as they passed each other while turning orders in to the kitchen and picking up food to deliver. She clearly enjoyed speculating about supposed backgrounds and motives to come here, and her chatter helped keep Kelly smiling, efficient—and awake.

Lang Elgin, one of the few male servers, joined in

now and then as he passed with food in his hands. Lang was a midforties guy whose paunch beneath his white shirt and dark pants suggested he enjoyed nibbling on the restaurant's food. He also joked about how the female waitresses got all the good assignments—like the ability to leave for a few hours. Kelly and Tobi just laughed at that, and Lang grinned back.

Kelly's shift was finished at seven o'clock, but at six forty, the cause of some of her stress walked right through the front door.

Fortunately, there were several tables available, many right near the restaurant's door. Kelly could only hope that if Alan intended to stay and eat, he would choose one toward the front, and not in her area.

When she noticed him, she had her arms full of burgers and salads that she was about to put in front of another group of people dressed as if for a business meeting—two women and a man. She served them with smiles and the right amount of attention, saying she would be back with more coffee.

But when she turned, Alan was immediately behind her. He had chosen a table in Kelly's section.

She felt the color drain from her face as her pasted-on smile sagged. She was going to have to deal with him again today, before she'd had time to think things through and determine how to act around him—if she had to again.

Well, now she had to. Immediately.

Fortunately, she had a good excuse for not taking his order right away. Instead, she went to get coffee for the table she had just left. The people there grinned and thanked her as she filled empty cups or warmed the brew left in other cups with a fresh top-off. Then she returned the nearly empty pot to where she'd picked it up, making her way through the still-filled tables and wishing that one of the other servers decided they simply had to have an extra tip, and would therefore take the order of the latest customer.

That didn't happen. It would apparently go against the servers' unspoken credo of fairness to one another, as well as Ella's official assignments. Alan's table was Kelly's privilege and responsibility for the evening.

When Kelly turned back again to approach her serving area, most everyone appeared to be eating, drinking or conversing, and in any case ignoring her.

But not Alan. He was watching her, the expression on his good-looking but unnerving face bland—yet Kelly couldn't help wondering what he was really thinking.

Sighing and pasting another false smile on her face, Kelly started making her way back to the tables she was serving.

"You okay?" Tobi, busing a tray of dirty dishes, was suddenly blocking her way.

Damn. It wasn't a good idea to appear as if she had issues at all here, not even with someone she hadn't known before and who might be a friend and kind of ally now.

"Absolutely." Kelly made a point of turning that fake smile into one she hoped looked real. "I'm just a bit tired after our visit to the plaza and helping there in addition to my regular shift. I'm not used to it—yet. But I'll get there. It was fun, and I really enjoy working here."

Was she laying it on too thick? Maybe, but Tobi just snorted a laugh. "It gets better," she said. "Or worse, depending on how you look at it. But if you need some help getting through the rest of today, let me know."

Really? She could just beg Tobi's help to handle Alan's order?

Kelly almost gave in to her impulse to say yes.

But although that might temporarily make her feel better, it wouldn't resolve any issues she had with the guy—assuming her worry about being here and exhaustion weren't the only problems.

"Thanks so much for the offer," she told Tobi, "but I'm fine. I'll take a rain check if we have another day like this one, though. Okay?"

"Sure." Then Tobi was gone, slipping between the filled tables toward the kitchen door. Lang was near there, too, apparently putting in an order.

It was time for Kelly to go take Alan's order.

Well, good, she told herself. He would likely be around as long as she was in town, and she simply had to learn to deal with him better.

"So what can I get for you this evening?" she asked as she reached his table. She hoped he would say he wanted nothing and just leave, but she knew that wasn't going to happen.

"Now that you're becoming a veteran server here and at Government Plaza, what would you recommend?" He smiled as he gave her a long, assessing—and hot— look that suggested he hoped she'd recommend sex with her.

Wasn't going to happen—even though parts of her body started churning in reaction to the thought.

Damn. What was it about this guy that got to her so much? He worried and unnerved her—but he also somehow turned her on.

Her mind grappled for a way to avoid seeing him again while she was here, but that would occur only if he stopped coming to the Haven. And she was sure that wasn't going to happen.

"Oh, lots of people say good things about our burgers," she said lightly. "I'm sure you've eaten them, though. What are you interested in trying?"

At his amused and even more suggestive look at her, she felt herself nearly melting onto the tiled floor. She hadn't meant to say anything that could be interpreted as the tiniest bit suggestive, but she had.

"There's a lot I'm interested in trying, but I think I'll stick with one of my standard sandwiches here tonight—a chicken club."

"Fine." Kelly took her notepad from her pocket and jotted it down, along with the kind of bread and sides he ordered. This wasn't too bad. She was acting appropriately as a waitress, and he was acting appropriately as a customer.

Before she left to put his order in, though, he brought her up short by saying, "Of course I know you don't serve alcohol here, but I'd love a beer later. How about you?"

Was he asking her out? She shuddered slightly as she looked him in the face and said, "Oh, I'm more of a wine person myself, but we don't serve that here, either. Sorry." That didn't exactly address what he'd asked, but maybe he would get the message.

"Very good. What time is your shift here over? If I've finished eating and left by then, I'll come back for you, and we'll go get you some wine and me some beer."

Kelly inhaled deeply. She didn't really want to deal

with this here while she was working. How should she handle it? "Sorry," she said. "When I'm through here, I'm just heading back to my place. I'm rather tired tonight." Although she hadn't told him to buzz off, she hoped he'd get it. If not, she would have to make it clearer if he asked her out again.

But his response made her freeze in fear, and not because she was scared of seeing him in any social capacity.

"I understand," he said, his voice quiet. "But I know who you really are, and you and I need to talk right away."

Alan had to hand it to her. Except for her initial split-second twitch of apparent nervousness, Kelly—her cover name, of course—maintained her cool demeanor.

She even managed a laugh as she said to him softly in return, "Now, that's a line I've never heard before. Let's see. I know who you are, too—Clark Kent. But I won't let anyone know that you're really Superman and likely to fly away soon."

"Good. I appreciate that. Now, what time do you get off?" He hoped that taking a firm stance would convince her to go along with him. He didn't want to even hint at threatening her with exposure around here to gain her cooperation. It was something he would never do, even if, as a last resort, he had to make her think he would.

He didn't take his eyes off her. She remained standing beside his table, but he could see her body tense as she squeezed the hand not holding her notepad into a fist. He figured she wanted to slug him or run. Or both.

But, smart lady that she was, she kept all emotion inside except for those few reactions he was watching for.

Beautiful lady, too. A lady who could probably use some support—emotional, and maybe also physical, since she appeared to sway just a little.

But then she seemed to get a hold of herself. "Hey, great idea." She smiled sexily at him as she leaned down and kept her voice somewhat low—although those around them might be able to hear it if they tried. "I'm new to this town and have lots of questions about it that I'm dying to ask a longer-time resident. I'm off in ten minutes. When and where should we meet?"

Kelly hated to play things this way, but it was part of the training pounded into her while changing her identity. Play along with things as much as possible if put into a compromising position. Never admit anything about yourself or your past.

Stay alert and always be smart.

So was this smart?

It was now seven fifteen. Sighing, wishing she could go the other direction, she instead pulled out of the Haven's small parking area for staff that was behind the restaurant. She headed carefully onto the wide city street, busy even at this hour. That was Blue Haven, with its active residents.

The car she drove had been given to her as part of her cover: a ten-year-old dull red domestic sedan that desperately needed a new paint job. Fortunately, it had survived its cross-country trip. She was a waitress not only here, but also where she had been placed by the Identity Division, in Baltimore. Restaurant servers didn't make much money, so an aging car, and as tiny and cheap an apartment as possible in this California beach town, helped her hide her real identity. Truth was, she actually didn't have much money except for her salary, even though the ID Division had provided her with an initial stipend to get her started.

Oh, the money she had saved while living here in Blue Haven and working in its best elementary school as a teacher was still hers. But it was in accounts under Shereen Alsop's name, and Kelly would dare to try using it again only as a last resort. What if Stan knew about those accounts and had paid their administrators off to let him know if Shereen tried to get into them?

Now, glad she had changed clothes before leaving, she drove only a few blocks in the opposite direction from the elite little town's civic center to the local bar that Alan had told her about, where they would meet, ostensibly for a date. He'd offered to drive her himself, but she wanted her own vehicle close by in case she felt most comfortable fleeing—after giving a good excuse, of course, like she was getting ill.

Which she might be, upon considering the impending meeting.

She had frequented Tony's Lounge now and then when she had been old enough after growing up in Blue Haven. Going there just added to her hurdles of potentially running into someone who might recognize her. Despite the chummy name, it was a lounge of renown around here, where many local politicos and businesspeople met after hours to toast deals they'd made that day with pricey drinks. Even elementary school teachers frequented it occasionally—especially one whose sister, a real estate broker, was married to a city council member.

Kelly pulled her car down the familiar driveway between Tony's and the Haven Liquor Locker beside it. Both were owned by one family, and Andi had been in the same high school class as the son, Tony Jr. Kelly knew him, but not nearly as well as her sister had, so she wasn't worried about him recognizing her.

The parking lot behind the bar was busy, but she quickly found a space.

Before she got out of her car, Alan was beside the driver's door, waiting for her.

She swallowed. Years ago, she had occasionally been on stage in high school plays. She knew how to act—and her acting abilities had been enhanced by the Transformation Unit instructors while her identity was changed.

It was time. She grabbed her purse from the floor in front of the passenger's seat.

When Alan opened the door for her, she smiled broadly and said, "Well, fancy seeing you here. Let's go get a drink."

Kelly had changed her clothing a bit from the garb she wore as a server, Alan noted while she matched her pace to his as they entered through the bar's back door. She still wore the same white blouse and somewhat uncomfortable-looking shoes, but she'd donned a longer skirt.

Theoretically, he supposed, that should make her appear less sexy.

It didn't. Kelly Ladd was one hot lady, no matter what she wore.

And despite himself, he couldn't help imagining how sexy she'd be wearing nothing...

She's become part of your assignment here, he reminded himself unnecessarily and shrugged off any inappropriate trains of thought.

He hadn't changed from his official uniform here—a suit. That was fine. He'd had his job with the CIU long enough to feel comfortably chameleon-like in what he wore, depending on the situation.

He hadn't been at Tony's often, but it always seemed crowded. And dark. And noisy.

Hopefully it was a good public place for the conversation they were about to have. One in which he intended to ensure that, no matter who the lovely woman with him was, or wanted people to think she was, they would work together for their common purpose.

"How about over there." Kelly pointed to one of the room's few empty tables. It was way off in a corner. There were plenty of other people around it, but there was something remote and impersonal and—well, promising about it.

"Looks good," he agreed, and used the excuse of maneuvering through the crowd in the darkness to take her arm.

The moment he touched her, she looked up at him, her eyes wide and wary. And then she grinned. "I have a feeling this evening is about to get interesting," she said.

"You got it," he agreed and, not letting go of her, moved in front so he could be the one to steer them through the crowd.

In a minute, they were at the small, square table. He did his gentlemanly thing again and pulled out the chair.

He took his seat across from her and pushed one

of the menus in the table's center toward her, keeping one for himself.

"Let the games begin," said Kelly, her smile this time appearing to challenge him.

"And may the best person win," he agreed.

Chapter 5

"So what would you like to drink tonight?" Alan looked across the table at Kelly with an expression that suggested he might want to drink *her*. Her shiver indicated both nervousness…and pleasure.

Under other circumstances, she might even enjoy flirting with a man like him.

But now, caution had to win out over any sexual interest. He was most likely playing her.

Well, she could do the same to him.

"Something nice and smooth and…tasty." She smiled at him in a way she hoped suggested she might want to taste him.

"Sounds good to me."

Their server came over. He wore a T-shirt and jeans and acted enthused enough that he was clearly hoping for a big tip. Kelly knew the type but had no problem with that, especially since Alan was apparently treating. She ordered a rich-sounding zinfandel, while Alan asked for an imported German beer. He also requested chips and salsa so they could nibble while they drank—and talked.

The volume of conversations around them was intense, which also provided Kelly with some relief. This could be considered a date between acquaintances, and no way could they have a heavy discussion here on any topic—just the way she liked it.

Not that she was certain what this meeting was about, but she could guess. Still, because of the covert nature of the ID Division and its assignments, even if Alan was who she believed he was, and he also knew who she was, they couldn't talk about it in this place.

The only way to hear much of what each other said here required at least some shouting, which increased the unlikelihood of getting very personal. Neither wanted anything of any importance to be overheard.

"So what made you decide to move to Blue Haven?" Alan asked loudly.

To save my nephew, for one thing, was the first response that flew into Kelly's mind. But she kept things simple, engaging in part of the lie she was supposed to use. "I come from the DC area and always heard how wonderful things are in California. This town sounded especially nice to me, and so far I'm enjoying it." That was a bit of an exaggeration, but it seemed to work. She regarded his truly handsome, angular face with a smile, her head cocked. "How about you? What brought you here—or are you from here originally?" She felt certain he wasn't.

"Kind of the same thing—I just heard interesting things about this area."

Their enthusiastic server returned with their drinks, and the rest of their somewhat loud conversation involved things Kelly would have preferred not talking about, like her background and life before she came here. But some of that was built into her cover, so it wasn't like she had to invent entirely new things—or anything she wouldn't want overheard. According to what she told him, she had been a restaurant server forever.

She also wondered how much of the story Alan told was true. He said he had grown up in Virginia, served in the US Army, and liked the military but not enough to stay in it. He had decided to go into private security, also in Virginia, and that was his experience before moving here.

Interesting. Believable, whether or not it was true. Kelly found herself relaxing a bit, as if this were a true date.

Not that she would ever let her defenses down. She couldn't.

Some of the tables around them emptied, then refilled. Kelly wondered how long they had already been there. She didn't check her phone for the time, but realized it was getting somewhat late. She kept nursing her wine, not wanting to order another—and not just because she had to drive back to her apartment when they were done.

No, she needed to stay fully alert.

But she almost spilled the small amount of it that was left when she heard a familiar voice behind her, talking loudly over the crowd.

It was Stan.

* * *

Alan had been enjoying their time together—especially since he had an agenda he hadn't told Kelly about yet. But he would when it was over.

He intended for them to take a short walk. Now that anyone paying attention to them would figure they'd been on a date, they could be seen together even more without suspicion about their real reason for seeing each other.

But now, he noticed Kelly wince at the same time he heard Stan Grodon's raised voice and guffaws as he marched into the lounge area with a woman Alan hadn't yet met.

From Alan's perspective, that was okay. To Stan, security guy Alan Correy should be just an ordinary fellow who also sought out sexy women to date.

But despite how Kelly quickly got a hold of herself, it was better if she didn't spend a lot of time in that man's vicinity.

Alan knew she'd been well trained, but she was only human.

Oh, was she human…and female…and sexy…

And Stan, standing behind her, had apparently just noticed her presence. He glanced down, away from his own attractive date, a blonde who was even more skimpily dressed than Kelly had been in her server outfit.

Under other circumstances, Alan might have leveled a challenging look at the guy who'd dared to zero in on his date. But he didn't want to do anything to jeopardize his ability to remain a security provider for Stan.

Time to get her out of here.

"Looks like you're done, right?" he said to Kelly. "I'll get our check."

* * *

Kelly felt relieved when, after paying their tab, Alan pulled her chair out for her, then grabbed her hand and led her through the crowd—right past Stan—and out the bar's back door.

She had to get over this. While she was here, she was likely to run into Stan in a lot of unexpected situations, and she had to maintain her cool.

He hadn't recognized her yet. Hopefully he never would—at least not until she had found a way to make him stop hurting Eli and pay for what he'd done to Andi.

When they reached the dimly lit parking lot, Kelly turned to Alan, planning on thanking him for the drink and his company and saying good-night, just as she would do on a date.

Instead, he smiled at her in a way she could only describe as grim, and said, "Let's walk."

She started to refuse, but he took her hand again, even more firmly this time, and started leading her past the rows of cars and toward the street.

"Anyone seeing us will just think we had a great enough time that we don't want our evening to end." His deep voice was low, but she could hear it just fine in the cool outdoor air. They soon reached the sidewalk by the bar and liquor store, and Alan led her to the left, in front of the bar. A roar of noise emanated from it, but the sound was muffled by the closed door. "But you and I are going to talk," he added, stopping to look down at her with as sexy a grin as she had ever seen. To get her turned on—or to make anyone watching them think they were actually attracted to each other?

Oh, Kelly was attracted to Alan, all right, but she didn't trust him.

What did he really want?

Apparently the games he'd mentioned previously were now about to actually begin.

Well, no sense just waiting for him to start. Kelly also knew how to play the game—or so she hoped.

"Great." She clutched his hand even harder. "So what do you want to talk about?"

"You, Kelly. And Shereen Alsop."

Even though she'd expected this, at least somewhat, she flinched—but didn't stop walking.

"Who's that?" she asked. Part of her training when provided with a new identity was to admit nothing, so she wasn't about to tell Alan she recognized that name. Her real name.

"That's good," he said. "You're at least complying with some of the instructions you were given. But you shouldn't have come here. That was completely against what you were told."

"Oh, really?" She kept her tone light. "I don't know what you're talking about."

The hand holding hers moved enough to swing her around, and suddenly Alan was looking down at her. Despite the lack of streetlight, Kelly could still see the anger on her companion's face.

"I... I..." Before she could figure out how to finish, his mouth came down on hers.

His kiss was startlingly sexy, and so was the way his body soon molded to hers.

Get away from him! something inside her screamed. They might be in public, where they could be observed, but nobody was near them now. She could be in danger.

And yet she didn't believe that. She threw herself even more into the amazing kiss.

When he finally pulled away, he said perhaps the last thing she'd have expected from him then. "Go home, Kelly. To your real home now, the one you were given."

She hesitated before answering. "I understand what you're saying and why." She ignored the absurd hurt she felt over him kissing her like that, then tossing her away as if it had meant nothing to him.

It should have meant nothing to her, too—just a means for them to continue pretending to stay in character here.

"Then—" Alan said.

But Kelly continued, her voice very soft and trembling. "I gather you're from the ID Division." She looked up into his face once more and saw him give a brief, curt nod. "And you clearly know who I am. You must know why I ran away in the first place."

Another nod.

"I came back here because I learned that my nephew, Eli—you've met him—he's in danger here, being abused by his father."

"If you're familiar with how the ID Division works, you know that I'm here to find the hard evidence against Stan that you weren't able to gather. I'll work on protecting Eli, too. But you need to leave."

"Not until I'm certain that Eli's okay." No matter who Alan was and what discipline he might be able to get the ID Division to rain down on her, she had to do this.

She had to save her beloved nephew, notwithstanding any consequences to herself.

"That's your final answer?" he demanded, still staring down at her.

"It has to be. I—"

He leaned down and stopped what she was going to say with another hot, incredibly wonderful kiss. This was ridiculous. This was wonderful.

Did he really think she'd start obeying him because she was turned on by him?

"Here's what we're going to do, then," he said, holding her close and whispering into her ear. "We're going to work together to find that evidence and bring Stan down. But if you're here, you're going to have to listen to me so I can both train you and protect you. Got it?"

He punctuated it with another kiss that took her breath away.

On one level, she wanted to shout "No!" and run away.

But on another level, she realized that two of them working directly together might be more effective than either of them working alone.

"Got it," she said and reached up to pull his head down to hers for another kiss.

This was merely adding to their cover, Alan assured himself as he finally pulled his head slowly back, away from Kelly's mouth. Her kiss. And then he took a step backward, too, to distance his body from her soft, enticing curves.

He had to think. To make himself remember a similar situation between a CIU operative and the person the ID Division was protecting that had worked out, even though the result of that case would be quite different from this one.

"As enjoyable as this is," he said, "and as helpful as it may be to ensure that anyone paying attention to us believes we're together now and thinks they know why, it isn't helping us accomplish what we need to."

"You're right." Kelly sounded breathless, but as he regarded her in the low light between street lamps, he saw that her smile was wry. "I agree that, since I'm staying here, we need to work together. Your main goal is to get proof against Stan, and I'm all for that. But my real focus now is to make sure Eli's okay, then I'll go after Stan."

"I get that." He reached out for her hand once more and started walking slowly down the wide sidewalk again, away from the bar since a few patrons had just come out. "And you're right. Young Eli needs a guardian angel."

She stopped, pulled herself in front of him. Her lovely face twisted into an expression of concern and fear. "What do you mean?"

Maybe he shouldn't reveal this to her here. Maybe he shouldn't reveal it to her anywhere.

But she had a right to know.

"There's actually a good reason for you to be here," he said in a tone that was more compassionate than the one he usually used. "Let's walk some more and I'll explain."

"No," she said. "Explain now."

He'd suspected it wouldn't be easy to work with this woman. For one thing, he had been affiliated with the military, and now government agencies, long enough to believe that orders were orders, and disobeying them only brought trouble. You could discuss them, maybe, depending on the circumstances and factors like time, in case there were better alternatives or ways to comply. But disobey them completely—never.

And here he was, about to risk his career to work with a woman who disobeyed a direct order that she'd had to expressly agree to in order to get the benefits and protections offered to her by the ID Division.

Yet as much as he disliked the concept, he could understand, under these circumstances, why she did it.

She needed to know that, and why he was actually considering making an exception in her case.

"This isn't the right time or place to get into detail," he said. "If necessary, I'll do so later, when we're truly in private and can talk."

"What?" she demanded, but at least she continued walking with him.

"Well...since I've been here I have seen indications that Stan Grodon isn't always kind to his son, Eli. I mean, I've seen—"

"That bruise on Eli's face." It wasn't a question but a statement, and Alan wasn't surprised she focused on that.

"Right. And more."

"Like what?" She snapped to a halt and stared up at him.

"As I said, we'll talk about it later. Right now, I'm just going to express regrets that I probably haven't handled this as well as I should have." He would never admit it to her—he even hated admitting it to himself—but his job here might become a little easier if Stan increased the cruelty to his son, particularly his criticisms while the city council security detail was in his presence. Alan had been around enough to observe some of that. And if the SOB did more, even if Alan hadn't yet found evidence he could use against Stan for possible murder, he might obtain enough to have him arrested for child abuse.

Then, maybe more physical evidence of what had happened to his wife could be found when Alan got the right to enter Stan's home to seek evidence of child abuse to keep the guy incarcerated for a while.

But really? He couldn't, wouldn't wish any more of that on the kid. He would find a way to succeed no matter what. And certainly would never admit to Kelly these cruel and nasty thoughts.

Even the idea would undoubtedly make her hate him enough to draw away immediately and refuse to work with him despite her own precarious situation.

Which would be justifiable, under the circumstances.

"What are you talking about?" Kelly demanded.

"Let's just say that, on reflection, I can see why Eli Grodon needs someone on his side, no matter what else is going on around him—and around this town. I'll certainly cooperate—" *now* "—but I'm probably not the right person to protect him. You, on the other hand, are—"

"The perfect person to protect him," Kelly said. "And you can be sure I will. Now—are we meeting somewhere away from here for dinner tomorrow, on a supposed date if anyone asks?"

"That's probably the best plan," Alan acknowledged.

"Fine." Without asking his permission, she turned, grabbed his hand and began leading him back to the bar.

He admired that she was, to some extent, playing the role he had created for her.

He only hoped she wouldn't come to regret it—and make their working together here for a somewhat common purpose completely ineffective.

He regained at least some hope after they hurried back down the driveway and into the parking lot behind the bar. Kelly dragged him along to right beside her car, where she reached up, pulled his head down and involved him in one heck of a long, hot and sexy kiss.

He liked that she sounded completely out of breath when the kiss finally ended.

He didn't do much better—especially when he couldn't help pulling her back into his arms and kissing her again.

For show, he told himself, even as his body, which had already responded, grew even harder.

But soon Kelly backed off once more.

"See you tomorrow," she said, then opened her door and got in.

Chapter 6

Kelly took her time starting her car, hoping it appeared to Alan that she was having a bit of trouble with the old and ailing vehicle—but it was mostly because she kept looking at him and smiling, even as she glanced beyond him to the door into the bar.

She hoped to see Stan, as foolish as that might be.

If she did, was she going to fling open the door and chase after him? Accuse him of doing horrible things to his own son, even though she didn't fully understand the implications Alan had made to the kinds of abuse Stan might be subjecting Eli to?

No. She couldn't do that. Besides, she knew from Eli's web posts—and that spot on his face—that things weren't great. Maybe what Alan had learned was just more of the same.

Much more than it ever should be…and she was going to fix it. Somehow.

For now, she made herself grab hold of her emotions and get the car started.

But she couldn't resist glancing again toward the bar door, just in case…

No Stan. Good. She would have to get her emotions fully under control so she wouldn't attack him physically or verbally next time she saw him, most likely at the Haven.

That was more his specialty, although subtly, very subtly—as he had done to Andi before she disappeared. Or less subtly to Kelly herself, despite her inability to prove it.

Plus, she intended to get more detailed information from Alan on the pretext, at least, of needing to know what Eli had recently gone through so she could find a way to fix it—despite being a stranger to him now.

Pretext? Not exactly. She definitely needed to know what was going on now. And as she'd considered before, if it took ruining her own cover to make things right for her poor nephew, so be it.

Okay. It was time. She opened her window and called to Alan, "Good night. See you tomorrow." She smiled and waved.

"Good night," he called back.

She blew him a kiss, staying in the character he was establishing for them, then backed out of the parking spot.

She pulled down the driveway between the two one-story buildings and onto the street. She took a deep breath, attempting to calm her nerves enough to proceed carefully.

The drive to the large Havenly residential development outside of town where her small one-bedroom apartment was located didn't take long. There was no traffic at this hour—not that Blue Haven had a lot of traffic even during rush-hour times.

Her building was one of four arranged in a square, with a parklike area in the middle. Her apartment was on the top floor, with a view not of the pretty center but of the sometimes-busy street.

Those apartments were less expensive.

She parked in the spot designated for her unit and sat in the car for another moment, trying to chill her nerves once more. Hey, she was home—or what passed for home now. She'd had a long, emotionally draining day, as most were since she had returned to Blue Haven. Although this was the worst so far, partly thanks to Alan and his non-confrontation of her.

Was he right? Could they work together? Should they make it appear to people here that they had a romantic relationship so no one would think it odd if they happened to chat with each other now and then?

Most of all, could she trust him? Work with him to bring Stan down? Allow him to help her ensure that things would be okay for Eli?

Well, she wouldn't figure all that out tonight. She exited the car with determination and entered the building, then headed toward her unit.

Trudging slowly up the apartment stairs, though, she couldn't keep her mind completely on track.

It kept returning to Alan.

Heck, he was one sexy guy. He knew who she was, and he'd admitted to being with the CIU.

Could she trust him?

Or maybe she should do what she had been avoiding all along.

Maybe, tomorrow, she would call Judge Treena to report in, accept the scolding that would undoubtedly occur…and ask a few important questions.

The next day started out very ordinary—or at least, despite its low points, as ordinary as any had been since Kelly's arrival back here in Blue Haven.

No breakfast visits from any city council members.

No orders to bring a large lunch to Government Plaza.

Boring. Worrisome. Frustrating that she wasn't accomplishing anything to help Eli, let alone find out what happened to Andi.

But that was part of the problem with going undercover like this. She had a role to play, as she did with the new persona that the ID Division had created for her.

She'd needed that to save her life.

She needed this one to possibly save her nephew's.

Which made her want to do something. Fast.

For now, though, she had to be patient. Somehow.

At the moment, she waited near the kitchen to pick up a large breakfast order for a group of accountants who'd come in to eat and discuss how to handle the next tax season for their corporate clients. Kelly had overheard part of their discussion and, as tired as she was considering how little she'd slept last night, she wondered if she would fall asleep right on her feet waiting for them to give her their orders.

But she didn't. She even gritted her teeth as she approached the table with some of the food, and managed to continue smiling and acting pleasant while the men in the mostly male group ran their eyes up and down her body, just like so many other male customers seemed to do.

It made her wish she could go back to her apartment and grab a sweatshirt and long pants while working this job.

Or maybe she should call Alan to come here and assume his role as her new guy-friend and make sure all the staring men around here knew it.

"Hey, sweetheart," said the next fellow she approached with a plate of eggs and toast. "I'd love a fresh cup of coffee now. Can you get it for me?" His gaze moved up her body toward her bustline, then back down to her butt.

Oh, yes, she would get him some coffee. But it would take every bit of her willpower not to dump it, steaming hot, onto his lap.

It was all she could do not to stomp off—at the very least.

But fortunately she had a way of dealing with this that shouldn't ruffle anyone's feathers—much. Not even her boss, Ella, could object. She looked around, then hurried away from this table and toward a line of booths along the front of the restaurant.

She had spotted her coworker Lang Elgin, dressed as usual in a white shirt and dark pants—same color combination, basically, as the women servers here, but definitely not sexy or feminine.

He could handle this table without being subject to any ogling, probably not even from the nearby women, thanks to his age and paunch. And Kelly definitely needed a break right now.

"Hey, Lang," she said after catching up with him.

"Could you take over that table for me for a while?" She nodded toward the group of chattering accountants.

"You need a potty break or a pincher break?" His wide grin bisected his round face, and Kelly just laughed.

"Guess," she said.

"That's fine," he said. "As you must know by now, I've been the backup for a lot of women working as servers here for quite a while." He leaned down toward her. "It's fine to ask me now and then," he said, "and I'm always good for it. But Ella, on the other hand…"

"I understand," Kelly said. "I won't ask you again… for another ten minutes." She smiled back at him, then told him who wanted coffee. She then headed in the direction of the restroom, willing to use that as her excuse.

No, better yet, she decided to use the back door and go outside. She had her cell phone in her pocket.

She had a call to make.

But Judge Treena didn't answer right away. And Kelly didn't feel comfortable leaving a message. Her burner phone number would undoubtedly show up as a missed call on the judge's line. Her Honor might call back soon, but Kelly needed to choose the time and place to talk to her.

Too bad she couldn't just erase her number now from Judge Treena's line. But, like the judge, she didn't have to answer a call as it came in.

The sound on her phone was already turned off. It was on vibrate. That was a good thing.

Had Alan already discussed her with Her Honor? Was he under orders to send her back? If so, he wasn't showing it—yet. But despite his suggestion that they work together, she couldn't trust him.

She returned inside quickly, headed for the restroom as her cover, then hurried back into the restaurant, where she signaled to Lang that she was back and ready.

"You okay?" Tobi asked. She had been near the front of the restaurant serving maybe a dozen tables. Kelly wouldn't have asked her for help anyway. Tobi, around her age but slimmer than Kelly, would have been subject to the same unwanted attention at the accountants' table.

"I'm fine…now." She glanced toward where Lang was walking around refilling coffee cups.

"I get it," Tobi said. The pretty server grinned almost wickedly at Kelly. "You mean flirtation isn't your first wish of the day?"

"Hardly." Kelly smiled back.

For the next couple of hours Kelly managed to do her duty, which was a good thing, especially when Ella emerged from her office and started issuing orders to her waitstaff.

No meeting at Government Plaza to attend to, fortunately, but a change in who was serving which tables.

Why? Probably just a demonstration by Ella of who was in charge.

Kelly was at the front of the restaurant waiting on the tables that were previously Tobi's purview when she felt her phone vibrate in her pocket. Since she had only recently bought her burner phone, hardly anyone had her number. She assumed it was Judge Treena, after seeing that number on her own phone.

This wasn't a good time to call her back.

Kelly ignored the vibration for now. She would, as she'd told herself before, have to choose when and where to try calling the judge again.

But the phone vibrated again almost immediately. Fortunately, she had just finished jotting down the orders of a man and woman seated at a booth near the door. She needed to go place the orders in the kitchen anyway, which she did.

After looking around to ensure that only the couple of cooks at this hour, two middle-aged guys, were in the kitchen, Kelly edged over to the wall and extracted her phone from her pocket.

The number it showed for the calls she had missed were not the judge's. No, she had traded numbers with Alan, and his showed up twice.

Was something wrong?

Surely he wouldn't be that persistent just to follow up on their plan to appear that they were attracted to each other.

As she stood there, her phone vibrated again. Yes, it was Alan.

Glancing around to make sure that Ella wasn't in the kitchen and that the two cooks' attention was on the stove, Kelly turned toward the wall and pushed the button to answer.

"Hi, Alan," she whispered into the phone, although she supposed that if the cooks heard her it wouldn't be the end of the world.

"Hi, Kelly. I'm starving. I need you to bring me a chicken club sandwich right away."

Really? But Kelly understood there must be an underlying message for him to make such a demand.

Right?

"Er... I'd be glad to if I can get the okay. The thing is—"

"The thing is there's a really good reason for you

to bring it to me. Now. And in fact, bring several. Different kinds are fine. There are some people here right now that I'd like to treat to lunch—and not just my security associates. Are you coming? It's really good timing."

And then Kelly finally understood.

Eli must be back at Government Plaza.

"Of course I'll bring over some sandwiches." Kelly's voice over the phone now sounded ecstatic. Clearly, she got it. "Chips, too. I don't think I'll be able to carry drinks, though."

"That's fine." Alan almost laughed, but at the moment he was in the small, desk-filled office that served as security headquarters in Government Plaza, and there were other guards with him. He had already figured that Kelly was intelligent and motivated, but she was also insightful and resourceful.

She clearly understood what he hadn't said.

"I'll be there as soon as I can." Then she hung up.

One hurdle met. The next was to make sure that those whose lunches would arrive soon remained to eat.

And talk, at least a bit.

"I'm going to take a walk," he informed his associates. Two women and one man, all dressed professionally in suits as he was, were huddled around one desk in their assigned room at the plaza, genially arguing about who was most likely to get hired first by a genuine government security organization, and not just work for this very nice—read that as schlocky—private security company. Their boss, Nevil Hancock, wasn't present so they could talk this way.

With Alan's genuine government security background, he doubted that any of them were qualified, but he wasn't about to tell them so. But their argument was a good thing, since they hadn't been paying attention to him. No one would expect their lunches to be delivered.

"I'll come with you," said Dodd Frankler. The senior guy hadn't been involved in that conversation, either realizing he might be too old or overqualified, or both, to worry about changing jobs just now.

He might expect lunch, or not. Either way, Alan would make sure he was happy.

He liked the guy, considered him an ally of sorts, though Dodd didn't really know who Alan was or why he was there—except to help out with security for the city council, which was fine.

Right now, Alan nodded at Dodd, stood and headed past the unoccupied rows of desks to the office door. After opening it, he checked both ways down the hall and stepped out.

Alan had last seen Eli Grodon when he was on his most recent patrol of the facility about twenty minutes earlier. Eli had been walking down the hallway upstairs that contained the city council members' offices, along with Cal Arviss, clearly his best friend. As they had passed Stan Grodon's office, Eli must have heard something inside since whatever conversation he'd been having with Cal stopped as his eyes grew huge and he hurried forward.

His father must not know he was here. Eli was probably on one of his quasi-internship missions that day and didn't want him to know.

Councilwoman Susan Arviss had been walking behind the two youngsters and helped usher them to her office. The hard glance she leveled on Alan as they entered looked both defiant and as if she was warning him not to say anything.

Of course he wouldn't. But he really did want to know what was up between father and son.

Would whatever it was help him to find the hard evidence of what had happened to Eli's mother—and prove, if it was true, that she had been murdered by her husband?

Without informing Dodd where he was going, Alan headed for the stairwell and walked up the flights to the building's fourth floor, where the council members' offices were, one story beneath the mayor's offices. That was part of what his detail did anyway, so it wouldn't surprise Dodd.

It was nearing noon, so many of the workers up here might already be out to lunch. Nevertheless, Alan started out in the opposite direction from Councilwoman Arviss's office and paused outside each closed door, listening.

That was part of their orders. They were to check things cursorily unless there was any evidence of a problem. If so, they were authorized to open those doors and ensure that all was well.

Or, if not, they were to make things well, which might include contacting the local police department.

Fortunately, nothing captured Alan's attention on the patrol. Even when they reached Councilwoman Arviss's office, he didn't hear anything, but he had a reason to enter anyway, so he knocked on the door.

In a few seconds, Cal Arviss opened it. "Hi," he said, sounding tentative.

"Hi," Alan said back. "Nothing's wrong." He wanted

to reassure the young man. "We're just doing some random checking—plus...well, can we come in?"

"Sure." Cal still sounded worried.

Eli sat behind the secretary's desk near the door. He didn't look up but continued to stuff envelopes with letters. His eyes shifted for a moment in Alan's direction and he seemed to take a deep breath, as if in relief.

What was wrong? Would Alan be able to find out?

"Can I help you?" That was Councilwoman Arviss, who stood up from behind her own desk and walked to the side of the secretary's desk where Eli was. She sounded pompous, in charge—and irritated at the interruption. But there was an expression in her eyes that made Alan wonder what she was really thinking.

He merely smiled. "I just wanted to let you know I've ordered lunch to be brought in from the Haven Restaurant for myself, plus a few more meals. I saw you arrive earlier and figured you might be interested in joining me. Okay?"

Cal was now with Eli behind the secretary's desk, and both their faces lit up. But they looked toward Susan Arviss for her okay.

"That's very nice of you," she said, but her tone sounded curt, as if she didn't believe that niceness came without a price.

Alan shot a glance at Dodd, who was now beside him also looking curious, as if he wondered what was really going on. Then he said, "I'm just very impressed by what you seem to be doing with these guys, Councilwoman. I had a mentor when I was about their age who did something similar, and I...well, I want to encourage you and them. So at least for today, I'm feeding you lunch and would love to hear even more about what you do."

And why everyone seemed so nervous when I first got here, Alan thought.

Plus, Kelly would get to participate at least some in this conversation—and might be able to get even more out of it about Eli and his father since she was in a better position to interpret than Alan was.

This seemed like a good deal for all of them.

He just hoped Kelly got here soon with their food.

Chapter 7

Fortunately, the restaurant wasn't extremely busy, maybe because it wasn't quite noon yet. Even so, Kelly did the appropriate thing and told Ella about the order for half a dozen sandwiches—she had rounded up to make it sound even better—that she had been asked to deliver to Government Plaza.

Ella was in her office. She always smiled at customers, but the intense look she leveled on Kelly, the standard in-charge expression she used for her staff, would have made Kelly wince if she had really cared about keeping this job long term.

On the other hand, she cared about keeping it for the short term. It gave her a reason to be here.

"I hope it's okay," she said to Ella, planning to do it even if her boss didn't like the idea. "I just figured it's another service we can provide more often to the people at Government Plaza, not just the council members, to promote the Haven even more. Maybe do it for the mayor and his staff one of these days. I know you sometimes have outside people make deliveries, but since you had some of us take care of that special council lunch yesterday, I thought this might be a good thing."

Ella's expression changed to one of amusement, or so it appeared to Kelly. "And it doesn't hurt that it'll give you a chance to see that security guy, Alan, again."

Kelly swallowed, wondering if her face was turning red. Hey, that would be a good thing, in keeping with the roles he'd suggested they take on.

"Well, yes," she said, giving a shy smile.

She wondered what Judge Treena would say about this angle, as well as Kelly's intended partial apology when she got hold of the judge. But not now. She would have to figure out a better time and place.

"All right, let's do it this time," Ella was saying, "although if it ever comes up again, be sure to check with me before committing to leave the restaurant, even for a short while. Okay?"

As if she had a choice. "Okay," Kelly responded. She couldn't wait to see Eli, and she might even get the opportunity to speak with him again.

She had put in the order at the kitchen before talking to Ella, so the two cooks had the half dozen sandwiches ready just a few minutes after she returned. "It's to go," she told them, "and I'll want a few bags of potato and apple chips to go with them."

Very soon, she was on her way. Noticing that Ella watched her leave, she didn't even take the time to change out of her serving outfit or use a scarf or sweater to cover herself up more. As much as Kelly would have preferred doing something with her attire, it was even more important that she not offend Ella at the moment, in case she had the opportunity to do this again. But once she got out of view, she pulled off the band she wore on her short, curly hair. If only she could do something now about her skimpy skirt...

The walk along the Blue Haven streets to the plaza didn't take long, and the entire time Kelly worried about how best to approach her nephew this time. Hopefully, once more, he would not recognize her.

She decided to wing it—again. She would be all bright and friendly and an excellent waitress who also had a thing going with the security guy. Oh, and she admired young men who did things to help their community. She hoped that had come across the last time she had seen Eli helping Councilwoman Arviss.

And if there was anything wrong in that particular young man's life, his relationship with his father, how he was being treated at home...

No. Of course that was number one on her agenda, but it had to remain deep inside her, invisible to others, at least until she figured out a way to fix what was wrong.

And she *would* fix it. Somehow.

Dodd had left the councilwoman's office almost immediately, but Alan had stayed behind. Now he sat on a chair in the corner of the room, out of the way, acting as if texting were taking up all his attention.

Not so. He surreptitiously watched the desk where the councilwoman sat at her desktop computer, reading something. No assistant or secretary was present, as seemed normal for these intern sessions. Fortunately, she didn't question his presence—the security guys seemed to be treated like general staff here.

Besides observing her, Alan also kept an eye on the table where her son—and Eli Grodon—sat stuffing envelopes. The two boys didn't talk much, and when they did it was in whispers, with their heads together.

Alan would have given a lot to hear them, but he suspected they were just trading boy talk.

On further reflection, Alan wondered if he had done the right thing, not only by hanging here but also by calling Kelly and ensuring she would come.

Sure, she wanted to see her nephew as often as she could. Even better, it would be good for Alan, and what he needed to accomplish here, to get Eli to reveal what was troubling him now—assuming the nice woman who couldn't act like his aunt could befriend him anyway and get him to talk.

Was he in more trouble with his father? Had Stan Grodon told his son to stay away from Government Plaza, and had Eli decided to defy him?

If so, then what were their respective motivations?

Most important to Alan was to find connections and more: the evidence he sought from the past. But Eli's current nervousness—and that bruise—made Alan certain something was also going on now.

It wasn't his responsibility to make sure the kid came out of this situation safely. But that was why Kelly had broken all the rules to get here. And his responsibility or not, Alan would do all he could to protect Eli, too.

Alan didn't believe in breaking rules. He'd seen what chaos that choosing not to follow orders could impose not only on those who disobeyed, but worse, on those around them.

He didn't want to see young Eli hurt, but the kid was in the middle of it all.

So were Councilwoman Arviss and her son. The councilwoman had apparently chosen to get involved, to help her son's friend. But did she have any idea what she might be up against?

Alan was here to find evidence that Stan Grodon was a killer. And those who killed would often do everything in their power to not get caught...even kill others who got in their way.

Well, Alan would do what he could to protect all of these people while fulfilling his own assignment.

And the fact that rule-breaker Kelly was in the middle of it? Lovely, sexy, lying Kelly? Even though, because she refused to follow rules, he should allow her to meet whatever fate Stan Grodon had in mind for Shereen, he knew he would protect her, too. And to do so—

A knock sounded on the office door. Susan Arviss jumped in her seat.

The two boys looked at each other with huge eyes. Fearful eyes. Expressions that suggested they both were concerned that Stan Grodon had found out they were there.

"I believe lunch has arrived," Alan said as Cal got to his feet to answer the door.

Kelly had breezed through the building's security with no trouble and now stood in the hallway outside Councilwoman Arviss's office, two large plastic bags in her hands.

When no one answered the door immediately, she

considered reaching into her pocket for her cell phone. Alan had said she should bring the food right here unless he texted her about somewhere else to take it. She hadn't gotten a text. But—

The door opened. Cal Arviss stood there. Kelly couldn't read the expression on the boy's round face, but it appeared flushed beneath his short brown hair, and perhaps guilty. Of what?

"Hi. I've brought your lunch." Kelly lifted the bags without handing them to the child. She wanted to ensure an invitation inside.

"Thanks." Cal reached toward her for the bags, but she pretended to misunderstand. She slipped sideways and edged her way through the door and past Cal. "Hi," she called out to Councilwoman Arviss. "Lunch delivery from the Haven."

From the corner of her eye, she saw Alan rise from where he had been sitting at one side of the room. So did Susan Arviss, who approached Kelly.

Were they both going to confront her so she'd have to hand over the bags without hanging around at all? She hoped not—especially since she managed a sideways glance toward the table where Eli still sat. He was the only one here who wasn't looking at her. That could be a good thing, although she doubted he would suddenly recognize her.

But as he looked down at the envelopes in front of him, she couldn't really see his face. His expression. Was he okay?

"Hey," she said, heading in the direction of the small table between the main desk and the one for an assistant. "How about if I help you set up this lunch? It's only sandwiches, but some really good ones." She made herself grin first toward Susan, then her son, and finally toward Alan.

She barely spared a glance in Eli's direction. She needed to act as if his presence were irrelevant, even though it was the only real reason she was here.

"It's okay," Susan said. "We can take care of it."

But Kelly had already reached the table. She put the two bags down on it and opened the first, smiling even though what she wanted to do was leave it there, rush to her nephew's side, hug him and ask him what was wrong and—

"Thanks for bringing it," Alan said. He'd pulled some cash out of his pocket to hand to her.

"Of course," she said. "Now, here are the selections." She emptied both bags, placing the sandwiches wrapped in plastic in a neat row, acting in her role as server. "We've got three chicken clubs and three roast beefs. Potato and apple chips, too." She extracted the small packages from the bags as well, placing one by each of the sandwiches. Only then did she look directly at Eli. She was seeing him for the second time in days! But she still did not know how best to help him…

"Which is your favorite, young man?"

He looked up slowly, not toward her but to the food. "Is roast beef okay?" he asked.

"Is that okay with the rest of you?" Kelly looked from the councilwoman to her son, but not toward Alan. She was sure he would eat whichever one was left.

"I want roast beef, too," Cal said, now standing by Eli's side.

"Chicken club is fine with me," Susan Arviss said. "But Mr. Correy placed the order. He should have first choice." She was holding out some money, too, so she apparently intended to pay for at least part of the order. Kelly suspected Alan wouldn't let her. And Kelly herself would be happy to pay for it all, now that she was able to be in the same room with Eli again.

If only she could just get close and talk to him... he still kept looking down, mostly, as if shy—or sad or in pain...

"We're good here," Alan said. "And in fact—you know what? One of those sandwiches is for my co-worker Dodd, and I'll have to find him and give it to him soon. But there's still one extra, so, Ms. Ladd, why don't you join us? Take a break from your serving, would you?"

Kelly tried not to look too ecstatic as she aimed her gaze toward Alan. Nor would she allow herself to worry—now—what Ella might say if she found out that Kelly stayed and ate part of the lunch she'd delivered here. At least it might just look a bit like they were romantically involved.

"That's very nice of you, Mr. Correy," she said. "Thank you. I'd be glad to, if it's all right with Councilwoman Arviss."

"Sure. Why not? We can make it a party." Susan, apparently buying into their facade, put down her money on the table near Alan, who pushed it back to her.

"My treat," he said. "Now, why don't we all sit down for a while?"

Alan watched as Kelly took a place between Susan Arviss and him, not directly beside the boys. She did sit across the table from Eli, though.

She unwrapped her chicken club sandwich and took

a small bite. "Mmm," she said. "This is good. I'm new enough at the Haven that I haven't tasted all its food." She looked toward Cal. "I've had a roast beef sandwich, though. I liked it. How about you?"

"Pretty good," the boy said. He finished chewing, then tore open his bag of apple chips.

"And what do you think?" Kelly did what Alan was sure she had wanted to do all along: address her nephew. "Have you had one of these sandwiches before, too?"

Eli nodded as he glanced at her, then back down toward the part of his sandwich sitting in plastic on the table. "I've eaten at the Haven lots of times," he said. "Good stuff."

The bruise Alan had noticed on the boy's face before was at least fading, and he saw no other indication of possible abuse. Unless he counted the quiet pain he read in Eli's expression, although he could just be seeing what he thought was there.

"Yes, it is," Kelly said. "I like working there." She paused. "And how about you? Do you like coming here and helping out like an intern?"

"Yeah, I'd like to do this even if I didn't get credit for it," Eli said. He appeared uncomfortable now. Because this was getting slightly more personal? He glanced toward Cal as if he wanted his friend to intervene and take over the conversation.

Kelly must have recognized his discomfort, too, since she immediately faced Susan Arviss. The councilwoman looked a little more relaxed than Alan was used to seeing her, her blond hair a bit unkempt, and she wasn't wearing lipstick. He figured she was in her early forties. She was attractive in a businesslike way, well-dressed and good at what she did.

"This is such a great program for kids," Kelly said. "They get to see a little bit of how the government works while they're doing something productive. Was it your idea?"

The conversation shifted to the concept of what the city could do for its citizens, even younger ones. Alan participated some, asking questions as they talked about whether other council members had bought into the program yet, and how schoolteachers and administrators reacted.

Cal piped in now and then, since he'd evidently talked to some of his teachers about what he had seen and learned here. Apparently, though, not many of the council members had started to participate in the intern program yet, and from Susan's attitude, Alan suspected she might sometimes be criticized for what she did. But she was encouraging others to do the same thing, and a few actually were.

Eli was quiet now, but Alan watched his gaze shift from Cal to his mother, and sometimes to Kelly or to him. He gave no indication of recognizing Kelly, which was good.

But this was her second time in his presence since her return. She was tempting fate, especially since she and her nephew had apparently been close at one time.

And Eli's silence didn't provide any insight into what was happening to him now.

Or anything his father might be into, good or bad.

"These guys are the only ones I'm working with right now," Susan was saying, "although a few of the other council members are doing a little, too. I hope to expand my efforts, including to kids whose parents don't work for the city."

"But that's the case with both of these kids, right?" Kelly asked, her face the picture of innocence despite what she clearly knew she was getting into. She looked at Eli. "And does your dad do anything like this?"

She was really pushing it, Alan thought. What did she think she'd accomplish?

And he wasn't about to mention how he'd heard Stan's nastiness toward his son a couple of times since his arrival here, when he'd seen them together in the hallway.

Eli said nothing, but took another bite of his sandwich without looking at her.

"Eli's dad doesn't have any interns right now," Susan said, her hard glance toward Kelly communicating that they weren't to talk about Councilman Grodon. She then started talking about some of the other council members who didn't participate in the intern program but took on other projects to encourage kids to get involved.

Alan realized that this meeting needed to end sooner rather than later—for young Eli's sake, and to prevent Councilwoman Arviss from getting upset with them, assuming she wasn't already. He waited till a slight lull in the conversation, then said, "Anyway, thanks for bringing lunch, Kelly. I'll walk out with you now so I can give the other sandwich to my colleague."

She glared at him, but only for a moment. "You're right. I need to get back to work." She stood, too, and her gaze circled the table. "Enjoy the rest of your lunch—and your afternoon."

Alan let her precede him out the door.

When the door was closed behind them, he said, "I have to go to the security office. Dodd will be there. Are you going back to the restaurant?" He said it firmly, as if it was an order.

She nodded, then said very softly, "I know I was getting out of line there. But I have so many questions…"

"We'll get answers somehow," he told her. "But this isn't the time or place."

He forbore trying to kiss the sad expression off her face.

"Will I see you later?" she asked.

"Absolutely." And then he turned to head down the hall. Maybe they could strategize then—or not. In any case, he would find a way to cheer her up, or at least he'd try.

Chapter 8

Kelly knew she had been pressing too hard. Too inappropriately. But she wanted so badly to get Eli talking about his father so she could learn what Stan was really up to these days.

How, and why, he had been abusing his own son.

Could she dare to get Councilwoman Arviss off on her own and ask her questions? She seemed to be on Eli's side.

But what if she reported Kelly's nosiness to Eli's father?

Just as bad, what if she decided to back away from Eli if she believed her kindness led local citizens to question her motives—and thus potentially result in political overtones?

No, Kelly wouldn't try questioning, or even attempting to befriend, Councilwoman Arviss—at least not now.

Slowly, Kelly started walking down the hallway to-

ward the elevator, but she only took a few steps before
turning to look back toward Alan. He had been there
for her, yet he hadn't let her go too far. She appreciated that.

She appreciated him—too much.

Why wasn't she surprised to see that he had also
turned during his walk down the hall and was looking at her? She had an urge to hurry back toward him,
past all the closed doors to the offices of city council
members, and into his arms.

That was the role they were playing, wasn't it? Only
it didn't feel like a role at the moment to Kelly.

She had to get her emotions under control. Remember that she wasn't supposed to trust him.

Hiding her sigh, though she realized Alan could
neither see nor hear it, she gave a slight wave with
her fingertips, then turned around again and continued walking.

Before she got to the elevators, though, one of the
office doors opened, and a small crowd entered the hall
near her. Though it was the far end of the hall from
Stan's office, he was among them.

Rather, he was in *front* of them, speaking boister-
ously about hurrying to the conference room downstairs for their meeting.

Kelly hung back, wishing the office doors were re-
cessed or that there was some other way she could hide.
But Stan saw her.

"Hey, it's that beautiful waitress from the Haven.
Hi…what is it? Kelly? Have you come to…serve us
again at our meeting?"

His tone and leer were both suggestive, and Kelly
wished she could make herself invisible. Better yet,

she wished she could slap the miserable wretch's ugly face with impunity. Or slug him till he promised to leave his son alone.

And admit to the world what he had done with his missing wife.

But attacking, or even offending, him now wasn't a good idea—not in her role as Kelly. Besides, the quicker he left this floor, the better. She assumed he didn't know his son was here, in Councilwoman Arviss's office.

Kelly smiled and said, "Sorry, but I've got to get back to my restaurant. But I hope you have a great meeting."

One in which everyone would see Stan Grodon for the heartless, selfish killer he was...

Not going to happen.

"Another time, then." With one hand in the air waving to her, his suit jacket sliding down his arm to reveal the long sleeves of his white shirt, he turned his back on her and hurried toward the elevator bank, leaving Kelly standing there inhaling deeply in relief.

At least this time she hadn't had to get any closer to the man she abhorred than several distant feet away.

She watched the crowd head for the elevators behind Stan, counting eight of them—five men and three women. They were all dressed as if for a city council meeting or something else businesslike. She saw a couple of the people from the lunch the other day, so she knew some besides Stan were on the governing council.

The mayor wasn't among them. He was the same man who'd been in office when Shereen fled town.

Who were the others?

One of them, a man, looked familiar. Very familiar.

In fact, she knew him from local news and otherwise, way back when, when she had still lived in Blue Haven. Back then, his commercial real estate business had been a highly advertised, attention-stealing competitor of the one where Andi had worked. Andi's had been the town's premier company, but this guy had obviously been trying to change that. He'd imposed his presence into the media all the time.

Remembering the circumstances, Kelly found herself almost gagging.

She had nothing to base it on except conjecture, but seeing the man in Stan Grodon's presence almost transported her back to that difficult past. It was when Andi had been championing a really nice piece of property owned by one of her company's clients, one in a commercial area not far from the beach, as a great place for the National Ecological Research Administration to open a local office.

Her sister had talked to Kelly—Shereen—a lot about how frustrated she was, and how important it was to her to complete the potential sale to NERA.

And how intense the competition was, since another local real estate company, the one owned by this outspoken, pushy man whose name Kelly finally remembered—Jerome Baranka—was promoting another site for the prestigious, and undoubtedly profitable, office.

Stan had turned his back on his wife and promoted Baranka's property in front of city council. Had he been paid off by the wealthy, unprincipled businessman? That had been Shereen's speculation at the time, and Andi had wondered about it, too, even as she struggled to do her own job and sell the site she represented—one she really thought better for the intended purchaser.

Unsurprisingly, Andi and Stan had argued about the situation and Stan's subversion, as well as other things. Andi had been so upset about the situation that she'd hinted to her sister that she'd documented concerns about her personal and professional life, and that she kept it with some information hidden in her house. And then Andi had disappeared.

Jerome Baranka was now—still—publicly in Stan's presence.

Kelly had a strong suspicion which real estate company had made the sale, though she had left before any deal was consummated.

Had that had something to do with what happened to Andi? Was she now in the presence of not only Andi's murderer, but also the person who had instigated, intentionally or not, what had occurred?

Clearly she couldn't ask. Neither could she allow herself to throw up while surrounded by these people, despite how her stomach churned and her senses reeled.

She turned and made herself walk at a decent pace as she headed away from them, down the hallway toward where she had last seen Alan.

She wanted to avoid him now, too. She imagined she must look as horrible as she felt, and she didn't want to answer any questions, not till she had found a way to calm herself.

I knew I'd see these people and others when I came back, she reminded herself. She had chosen to come here nevertheless. But at the moment, that thought failed to help her cope with her hopeless mood.

There was a lit exit sign over a doorway at that

end of the hall, and she assumed it was an emergency stairway. That was where she headed, and she pushed it open slowly, just in case it somehow had an alarm attached, even as her mind scrambled for a reason she would give if she were caught.

Fortunately, there was no alarm. The doorway led to a set of steps heading both up and down, and she hurried into the stairwell to flee downward, wanting to leave the building as soon as possible.

If only she could leave her thoughts behind here, too, she wished, as three flights down she finally reached bottom and pushed open the outer door to the alley behind the plaza.

At least she could breathe here.

But could she continue this afternoon and beyond in her assumed role as a server who knew nothing and no one in this town?

She had seen Eli again. She had to focus on that and nothing else at the moment, except that she had to find a way to help him.

She kept telling herself that as, straightening her shoulders, she started trudging down the alley in the direction of the Haven.

Where she would return as Kelly.

But for now, she knew of no way to help her sister—or her nephew.

What was wrong?

From the security office where Alan now sat with Dodd, he had seen Kelly appear in their end of the hall, after he had encouraged her to leave the building. Agreeing, she had headed toward the elevator bank.

Instead, she had apparently left via the stairway.

What was she up to? Was she trying to investigate something here, in the plaza?

Not a good idea for a waitress to act so snoopy.

"Just thought of something I need to check out," he told Dodd, standing at the desk where they had been discussing the meeting scheduled to start in the downstairs conference room in about ten minutes. They would both attend and ensure that security was maintained.

That gave Alan a few minutes, at least, to try to figure out what was going on with Kelly.

"You go ahead if I'm not back in five," he continued, detecting amusement on the more senior security guy's face, as if he, too, had seen Kelly and figured out why Alan was leaving. If so, he was right—but he didn't know it all.

"Will do, bro," Dodd responded. "Have fun—but don't be too long. The meeting we need to monitor is going to start soon."

Alan just grinned as he left. He looked both ways in the hall before he crossed to the stairway entrance, then headed down.

At the bottom, he pushed the door open and scanned the alley. A car drove by, and he saw a couple of cats near a garbage can, but no sign of Kelly.

Even so, he went in the direction she'd have headed to return to the restaurant, down Main Street. Maybe there was nothing wrong, though her going this way sparked concern in him.

He hustled from the alley and onto the street in time to see Kelly crossing at the next intersection. She only had another couple of blocks to go to reach the Haven.

And he had that meeting to attend—and act as one

of the security team. It wasn't likely he'd learn anything useful, yet he had to be there.

At least Kelly seemed okay. He would talk to her later to find out what her exit that way had been about.

Instead of returning to the building through the alley, he turned and headed back to the main entrance—in time to see Councilwoman Arviss exit with her son and Eli. Obviously, whatever the meeting was about, it wasn't for all council members.

"Seeing these great helpers back to school?" he asked her.

She nodded, then glanced back up the steps as if to ensure they weren't being followed. "They're done with lunch, and this seems like a good time for it," she said.

"Yeah," Eli agreed, and Alan couldn't help wondering if the boy knew his dad was now in a meeting and therefore unlikely to run into him.

He'd had some major concerns about the kid even before Kelly's illicit arrival in town.

Now he had even more.

"See ya," he called as the group headed down the street in the opposite direction from where Kelly had gone...and he meant it.

Okay. She had to be cool. Practical.

On her walk back to the restaurant, Kelly texted Alan that she looked forward to seeing him later, maybe for dinner.

He might already have some information about the dispute between Andi and Stan over the real estate angle, since Kelly had told her handlers at the ID Division about that possible reason for Andi's disappearance. They could have passed it along to him to help with his undercover assignment here. But she wanted to let him in on this latest information.

She didn't hear back from him immediately and figured he was probably at that meeting on his security watch. That was fine. She felt certain she would hear from him eventually, and then they would talk.

She had the time to talk to Judge Treena now if she could reach her, but she decided against it. Her nerves were frayed enough at the moment without having to defend herself the way she would to Her Honor.

A couple of police cars drove by, but all seemed well in this popular area. Once Kelly reached the Haven, she let Ella know she was back and handed over the cash Alan had given her for the lunch.

"Good job," Ella said, making Kelly smile a little. At least she had done something right, and making her boss happy, even for this brief moment, felt good.

Then, as much as possible, she shrugged off the rest of her fragility and anger and all the other emotions that had swept through her on seeing Baranka in Stan's presence—not to mention spending a little not-so-quality time with Eli—and transformed herself back into her role here as a server.

The rest of the afternoon passed quickly. And smoothly. They were busy but not overly so, so she was able to move her mind from everything else, at least somewhat.

Despite all the care she was taking to change her mood, it must have shown somewhat since Tobi, and particularly Lang, jabbed at her every time they could—good-natured teasing that she knew was designed to cheer her up.

She shot gibes back at them, even as she wanted to

thank them, even hug them, for being so nice to her. Or not nice, as the case might be.

Kelly was careful not to mention to Ella that she'd been gone as long as she had because she had joined their customers for lunch. It would negate the tiny bit of praise Ella had given her earlier. Ella had rules that she imposed on her staff, and fraternizing with customers like that during business hours was frowned upon, even though being friendly to them—and even flirting with them in those sexy uniforms—was just fine despite the contradiction there.

Though Ella did comment about the length of her absence, Kelly said simply that she had helped to serve Councilwoman Arviss and her guests, without mentioning who those guests were—or that she stayed for a while.

She kept her phone in her pocket. She wasn't surprised to feel a vibration at a time she wouldn't have chosen, when she and Tobi were taking orders at a table of two senior couples whom Ella introduced as some of her parents' closest friends—in other words, they were to treat these seniors like family, take good care of them and make Ella proud.

"Yes, our chicken potpie is wonderful," she told the elderly gentleman she had been waiting on, even as the tingling vibration at her hip stopped. "It's made fresh, of course, and our customers always rave about it."

"Have you ever tried it?" the man asked, aiming a squinting gaze up at her.

She'd tasted some of the filling, though not the crust, so it wasn't a complete fib to say, "I sure have. Wonderful!" she repeated.

"I agree," Tobi added from across the table. "It's

one of our best customer favorites." The other server winked one of her pale hazel eyes at Kelly.

"Let me have one, then," the man said, nodding with a firm expression on his lips that suggested he had made the most important decision of the day.

"I want to change my order," the other man said. "I'll try that pie, too."

"Of course." This time Tobi's expression was an exasperated eye roll that made Kelly want to laugh. But she held it in.

In a minute, they had finished taking the orders, and both hurried toward the kitchen to let the busy chefs know.

"What a group," Tobi said, her voice lowered. "No wonder Ella likes them. They're like her—full of orders and changes."

"Exactly." Kelly was hoping to slip away for a minute after they'd turned in the orders so she could check her phone, but she had the impression that Tobi was in a chatty mood.

Fortunately, though, once they were in the kitchen and the chefs had gone over the orders and promised to get to them right away—after Tobi informed them about the priority of these particular customers—Lang came in.

"Just got a big group in the front," he said. "I've already moved tables around, but I need some help." The paunchy server looked from Tobi to Kelly and back again.

"I'd be glad to," Tobi said, just as Kelly had hoped.

"Me, too, but not for a few minutes," Kelly added.

"Sure," Lang said, then turned and waddled out the kitchen door.

Tobi hurried to catch up with him.

Kelly headed down the hall toward the ladies' room.

No one else was there, so Kelly immediately removed her phone from her pocket. She opened a text from Alan: Lunch and dinner together on the same day? Sounds great to me. I'll bring takeout to your place at 7:30. See you then.

She felt a huge grin spread over her face. She was definitely getting together with Alan. All business, of course. They had a lot to talk about, even though he might not realize it.

Takeout at her place? He hadn't asked her to text her address. But Alan was undercover. In security. He undoubtedly knew where she'd lived before, when she was Shereen. He'd also be aware of Stan Grodon's address. So was Kelly, of course—unless Stan had moved Eli and himself away after "losing" his wife.

Maybe Kelly should find out about that. She obviously couldn't ask Eli, although she wanted to—and if they'd moved, to learn what her nephew thought about it. She would try to ask him that subtly sometime, somehow...

But for now, she could ask Alan where they were living.

And Alan, being who and what he was, most likely already also knew where the woman now known as Kelly lived. She'd test him by not providing the information unless he asked for it, though she suspected he wouldn't.

But she would see him that night. That was the important thing—for her safety. Her peace of mind. Her happiness of the moment.

She was absolutely looking forward to it.

Chapter 9

The meeting was over at last. Alan stood in the hall-way outside the conference room at one side of the door as the occupants exited, talking to one another but ignoring both him and Dodd, who was at the other side of the door.

Alan had done his official Blue Haven security thing and, with Dodd and others, kept close watch on the hallway outside the occupied conference room as well as the room itself.

He'd communicated off and on with their boss, Nevil, and other members of the security detail via cell phone to confirm that no one saw anything out of place. He had even talked to the Blue Haven police chief, Arturo Sangler, in coordination.

More important—to him—he had listened to what was going on during that meeting whenever possible.

There was nothing exciting, unfortunately. He didn't know who all the players were, except for Stan Grodon and a couple of other city council members—both men with loud voices and opinions they clearly wanted everyone to hear.

And the other participants? Men and women in suits who appeared to have businesses in Blue Haven. But nothing particularly noteworthy was brought up at the meeting—just some upcoming events like a county fair and a separate proposed music festival.

They obviously all knew one another so there had been no introductions, at least none Alan heard. Maybe it would have been more interesting if he recognized the people and the business interests they represented. Presumably, Grodon and the other city council folks were wooing local businesspeople in the hope they'd contribute lots of money to those proposed, and undoubtedly costly, events. Maybe to their next political campaigns, too.

But to Alan this was a waste of time, at least when it came to his real reason for being here.

It had been a kick, though, to trade text messages with Kelly, despite having to be careful when he read hers and responded. It was one thing for a member of the security detail to talk on the phone or text with others on the job, but he didn't want anyone to catch him doing something considered unacceptable—a black mark against his reputation here. To do it all, he needed to be perfect, or at least appear that way.

But he'd worked it out, and now he had something to look forward to—for the sake of his real mission.

The fact that he was meeting Kelly for dinner very soon—alone, at her place—well, that was a perk of sorts, but he reminded himself that their apparent relationship was simply part of both of their covers.

No matter how attracted he was to the woman, he never forgot that she had done the one thing he found intolerable. Kelly had broken promises and disobeyed orders, even though she thought she had good reason to.

Instead, she should have asked for help.

He would need to keep that in mind when he was with her that evening.

Kelly wished she knew what kind of takeout food Alan was going to bring to her apartment. Not that it mattered. But she had just gotten home about ten minutes earlier, removed the headband she usually wore to control her hair at work and changed into comfortable dark slacks with a lacy brown top she particularly liked—especially because its neckline was low but not revealing. She was now fussing around the one-bedroom apartment's small kitchen, where a table for two was located.

She had set the table with napkins, flatware and water glasses. She wished she had a bottle of wine. Would Alan bring that, too?

She still hadn't heard from him except to confirm he would be there around seven forty-five, ten minutes from now. He didn't ask her address.

Now it was her turn to get ready for him.

For their business meeting, she reminded herself. Never mind that it was private, in her apartment, or that they wanted to give the impression to anyone paying attention that they were an item, or—

A buzz sounded from the intercom. Kelly hurried out of the kitchen and through the tiny living room with its small sofa and single chair, toward the door. She pushed the button.

"Yes?" She tried to sound calm and relaxed, as if she weren't all excited about the idea of spending time with Alan that evening.

"Hi, Kelly," said a deep voice in response. "It's Alan."

"Oh, hi. I'll buzz you in. I'm on the third floor, apartment 322."

"I know," he said. "Be right up."

Opening the front door after Kelly's buzz, Alan glanced around. The moderate-sized apartment building's lobby was empty and seemed standard: white plaster walls, linoleum floors, high ceilings and one wall lined with mailboxes. There was a scent of cleaning fluid, so apparently the place was well maintained.

Pretty much what he'd anticipated.

He walked up the two flights of stairs to the third floor, two plastic bags containing their dinner in his hands.

Knowing that her name—now—was Kelly Ladd had given Alan all the information he needed to find her local address on one of the secure locator sites he had access to on his phone, thanks to being part of the Covert Investigations Unit. He figured that Judge Treena knew Kelly's location, too, but was silently giving Alan latitude to find and work with her—for now.

He'd also taken the time to check out the neighborhood on another of his resources. There were few reports of illegal activities around here—a break-in several months ago at a complex down the street, a couple of domestic disputes in this building, a car break-in nearby. Nothing major, and nothing to indicate this was a bad area to live in.

On the other hand, it was a far cry from the upscale neighborhood where Shereen Alsop had lived, and way below the elite area housing Stan Grodon and his son ...and where Andi Alsop Grodon had formerly resided with them.

He turned right at the top of the steps and headed toward the door to the second apartment, number 322. There, he pressed the button and heard the buzz from inside.

He heard the sound of footsteps, then the door opened.

Kelly smiled up at him, her brown eyes twinkling. "Ah, Mr. Deliveryman. Come in."

He wondered now what color her eyes really were, since most subjects helped by the Transformation Unit portion of the ID Division were given contact lenses as part of their makeovers.

Maybe he would find out someday, but not now. "Yes, Ms. Consumer. I hope you like Chinese food. I thought I'd bring something different from usual US fare that you're generally surrounded with at the Haven."

He glanced around the inside. The door opened into a small living room area, and he saw a couple of other openings he assumed led to the kitchen and bedroom. The furnishings were standard, a small tan upholstered sofa and chair both facing a shelf containing a flat-screen television.

Fair surroundings to live in. Impersonal enough for someone who wasn't a real person, exactly.

"Sounds great," Kelly said. "Come this way. I'll show you the kitchen." She moved away from him, one hand beckoning him to follow. Which he was glad to do, watching her back end swaying enticingly as she preceded him. No longer was she in that slutty, though attractive, waitress garb. Her outfit went well with the furnishings' coloration, in deeper brown. Her pants fit snugly, and her top? It was loose but hugged her curves.

Plus, he enjoyed her curly hair freed that way.

Good thing they had both agreed on pretending to have a relationship. He could stare at her as part of their cover. Although here, in private, they could act like the disinterested collaborators they were.

But staring at her, at least from behind, still worked for him.

He was glad, though, that he'd taken the time to change from his standard security uniform of a suit into a plaid shirt over jeans—more casual and friendly. And friendliness here wouldn't be a bad thing.

"Here we are." She pointed to a pale wood table that would fit two comfortably, though not more. The rest of the kitchen was tiny, too, with all the standard stuff but smaller: a metal refrigerator with the freezer part on top, a sink with counters beside it that didn't extend very far, although the right side held a compact microwave oven. The cabinets matched the wood of the counters.

To Alan, this did not look like a place to live for very long, even though he figured most of the building's low-rent tenants stayed for years.

"Great." Alan put both bags on top of the table, hearing a slight *thump* as the wine bottle touched the surface. "Do you have any wineglasses?"

The smile on her lovely face grew even wider. "I sure do. Wine sounds wonderful tonight."

And she looked wonderful tonight. He had a sudden

urge to move around to where she was now reaching into the cabinets above the counter to the left of the sink and extracting a couple of long-stemmed glasses.

Not that he wanted any kind of reimbursement for tonight's meal, but he suddenly craved a thank-you kiss. Or a kiss for any other reason. Or no reason.

"I've got something to tell you about Stan Grodon and that meeting this afternoon that might give you another angle to look into to find evidence about what happened to Andi," Kelly said, putting two glasses on the table. "Do you need a corkscrew?"

"Yes," he said. "That would be great." And so was the reminder about why he was really here—not to see this gorgeous and sexy woman socially, but to work with her for their mutual purpose of bringing down the man who had most likely killed her sister.

She turned her back once more and reached into a drawer near the sink, extracting a wine-bottle opener. It looked generic enough to have come with the apartment, since the place appeared to have been rented furnished and perhaps even with dishes and flatware.

Alan wondered what Kelly had told the leasing agent about where she'd come from, and why she was here, not to mention how long she was staying.

"Want me to do it?" She looked at the bottle Alan had placed on the table, food containers beside it.

"Let me." He reached out, and she placed the corkscrew into his hand.

"Yes, sir, Mr. Deliveryman." She laughed, then got some serving spoons from another drawer. She had already put plates, forks, knives and napkins onto the table so they were ready to go.

In a few minutes, they were sitting at the table, facing each other. They both had Chinese food on their plates: kung pao chicken, fried rice and stir-fried vegetables. Alan lifted his wineglass in a toast.

"May we find all the answers we need to suit both of us—and make Judge Treena happy, too," he said, staring into Kelly's pretty brown eyes to gauge her reaction to the latter. What did she think of Judge Treena—and making her happy?

"I'll drink to that." Kelly lifted her glass and took a sip. "Although I haven't talked to her, I suspect that if I asked Judge Treena what I could do to make her happy, she'd insist on something I'm just not ready to do now."

"Like move back to the location and job where she placed you? Maybe obey a few orders?" Alan knew that his wryness had an edge of irritation to it. All that had been done for Kelly had been intended to keep her safe. Now here she was, practically mocking the ID Division. And Judge Treena.

"I only wish I could." The sorrowful expression that suddenly washed over Kelly's face almost made Alan feel sympathetic. "But that's one of the things I want to talk about tonight. I said I have some potentially helpful information for you, and I do. But first— seeing Eli haphazardly that way, not really being able to talk to him or learn what's going on or how to help him… I need for us to discuss some kind of plan for me to fix things for him. And if you want to help, too, that would be fine."

Kelly watched Alan's face change from hard and maybe even angry to pensive. She was challenging him, sure, but it was within his purview as a CIU agent to help her with what she had asked.

Would he? She really hoped so.

"I understand that's why you've come here, Kelly," he finally said. "And why you felt you had to break every promise you made to get the Identity Division to help you. But—"

"But you don't really get it." She looked down at her plate rather than at him, keeping her tone level, trying to swallow her disappointment.

They'd talked some about becoming allies, working together toward their important and related goals. Well, she absolutely wanted him to achieve his: finding compelling evidence to convict Stan of doing whatever he had done to her sister.

Did he want her to achieve hers—convicting Stan, and even more pressingly, helping her nephew?

"I do, Kelly. Definitely." His voice was soft now, and when she looked back up at him, his deep brown eyes captured hers in a glance that truly did appear sympathetic.

But he was part of the Identity Division. Everyone affiliated with the agency, particularly the Covert Investigations Unit, was a good actor. It went with the territory.

He stood up then, crossing his arms in front of what she knew was a hard chest. "I realize you don't necessarily believe me, but I've been keeping an eye on young Eli every time I see him in Government Plaza and elsewhere. I don't know about mentally, but he didn't appear physically abused until the last few days. I've made notes and taken photos when I could. When I get the evidence I need on his father, I'll be able to take him out of the picture. Even before you showed up here, since I knew his history—and yours—I assumed

I'd be able to turn him over to his aunt eventually. But your being here changes things, and could make it even more difficult for me to deal with Stan Grodon."

"I… I didn't want that." Kelly melted downward into her chair. This entire situation had always been hard for her. It had to be a nightmare for Eli, and when he'd felt bad enough to hint about it on social media, she'd felt compelled to forget her own needs and come here, to help him.

But she also wanted to make sure Stan Grodon was taken down, as he should be.

"Of course you didn't." He looked as if he might stride toward her and she tensed, both wanting him close and hoping he wouldn't get near her. If he tried to comfort her by holding her, she was afraid she'd fall apart.

Instead, he seemed to hesitate for a few seconds, then resumed his seat. As if he had not stood at all, he took a sip of wine and began eating again.

Kelly took the opportunity to tell him about having seen Jerome Baranka with Stan that morning, heading for the meeting. She described the situation before her sister had disappeared: the real estate mogul, his apparent friendship with—bribery of?—Stan. Stan's arguments with his real estate agent wife.

"I knew some of that," Alan said when she was done. He'd finished his meal and looked across the table toward her, his craggy dark eyebrows furrowed. "I'd looked into Baranka Real Estate when I first got here, and they were on my list to check out further. But from my initial investigation, that real estate angle was only one of several possibilities, and Stan and Baranka weren't in as close contact as Stan was with some others on my list. But you can be sure I'll examine that transaction more closely now. Not sure it'll yield anything solid in the way of evidence against Stan, but we'll see."

"To me, it still seems the most likely possibility," Kelly said. She hadn't finished her dinner, mostly because she wasn't really that hungry, not with all the emotional mental flogging she'd been doing to herself.

No. It was her brother-in-law's doing. And she really did need to help her nephew.

She took a long swig of wine, then looked across the table intently at the man who was here to bring Stan down. "Look, Alan, I know you're mad at me on behalf of the ID Division, and maybe otherwise, but we've already decided to help each other. And first thing, I have to make sure Eli's okay. You see him more than I do, and I appreciate your giving me notice so I can pop in on him at Government Plaza. But...well, I've been contemplating trying to become Councilwoman Arviss's good buddy so I can hang out with her more, but have a lot of reservations about it. There's got to be some way for me to get closer to Eli, and I've wondered if she's the key. What do you think?"

"Bad idea, at least for now," Alan said. "She seems to be a strong and helpful presence in Eli's life. If you press her, question her, she might ask too many questions, of Stan and of you. I'll try to sound her out if I get the opportunity, but you should avoid her for the time being."

"Okay. You're right. That's kind of what I decided. I don't want to ruin her acting as a friend to Eli. He needs someone in his corner. He's probably suffering..." Kelly hadn't meant to raise her voice like that, but everything she had been holding inside suddenly erupted. Still staring into his handsome face, she tried to figure out what Alan was really thinking… before she felt tears start dampening her own cheeks. "I… I'm sorry," she said, again looking away from him.

"Me, too." Alan's voice was gentle—and it came from beside her. "I wish I had a magic solution for you. Or that I'd found everything I was looking for to bring Stan Grodon down so you didn't have any reason to come here. But I didn't. And we have to go from here."

"I—I just thought I'd at least figure out a way to see Eli more while I'm here, to help him," she blurted. "But everything I come up with could hurt him—and maybe me—more."

She felt a touch on her shoulder and turned to see Alan right beside her. She rose, he pulled back her chair, and suddenly she was in his arms.

She hadn't meant to cry. Not at all, and not like this. But she felt as if all the fear and stress she'd been holding inside was now erupting, and that it was okay since she was being held by the one person who, even if he didn't agree with her, understood best what she was going through.

She stood there for a minute getting herself back under control. Or trying to. At least the tears stopped flowing.

But she realized she liked where she was—being held by Alan, comforted by him…and more.

Her body started tingling, reacting to him in all the most sensitive places. He was one sexy guy.

But that wasn't appropriate. She needed to get away from him. She moved to look up at him, tell him she was fine…and wound up looking right into his eyes.

They were blazing with desire. That stimulated her even more. And when his mouth came down and met hers, she was ready for it. More than ready.

She realized she had been waiting, hoping for this as the kiss grew deeper. Hotter.

Waiting for this—and more.

Chapter 10

Alan hadn't intended to kiss Kelly. To touch her like this. He had only wanted to soothe her, yet he was affected by the way she looked at him. Seemed to wait for him. To want him…

She tasted wonderful, slightly spicy like their dinner. He tested her taste even as he teased her tongue with his.

Her breasts against him felt warm, curvaceous. And when he reached down to grasp her bottom, pull her closer, he nearly gasped with pleasure as she pushed against his erection, hardening it.

What would she be like naked…?

She must be thinking the same as him, since her hands were suddenly at the back of his shirt, lifting it, touching his flesh with her soft, exploring hands. And then they dipped lower, as if she wanted to grasp his butt as well, but not through his pants. Inside them.

But as he moved a little to help her, to start removing her clothes first, she pulled back and gave a small laugh.

"Hey, this may be the role we're playing in front of people, but for real?"

The role. Pretending to be attracted to each other so they could be together in public, sharing where they were, talking to each other, without anyone suspecting, hopefully, what they were really about.

The thought that he wasn't the first CIU member to come up with this plan rocketed suddenly through Alan's mind. He had wound up helping at the end of that other agent's assignment, seeing him with the woman he'd needed to help, recognized that their attraction to each other might have started as a role but had morphed into reality.

Would that happen between Kelly and him? No way. Too many differences between them, in attitude and more.

Alan pulled back a little, his breathing uneven, then stopped. He wanted her. No matter what or why. He grinned down at her gorgeous face, her teasing smile. Her challenging, sexy eyes. "We can always rehearse when we're by ourselves," he said. Then he didn't want to talk anymore.

He reached toward her, moving his hand inside her flowing, low-cut top until he could grasp one full, firm breast over her bra, then the other. He kept his eyes on hers, though, knowing he would make himself stop if that was what she wanted.

"Rehearsal sounds good," she said in a husky voice. And when she reached out to grasp his erection through his pants, he knew they were a go.

* * *

Kelly felt as if all her concentration was on her breasts, where Alan touched them. Teased them. Brushed, then gently squeezed, her nipples.

"I think this rehearsal needs to move into the bedroom," she managed to say, even as she continued to gently cup the area where his arousal extended his jeans, wanting to rub it harder. To feel its flesh.

Maybe even to taste it.

This was so strange. She'd had relationships on and off while living here before in Blue Haven, but none since she had shed her old persona and become Kelly.

Now, for the first time in forever, Kelly craved sex. Not just any sex.

Sex with this man.

"I agree." Alan's voice was raspy, but he backed away enough so she could no longer reach him. Nor was he still touching her breasts.

"This way," she said immediately.

Was she being foolish? Could be, but sex wasn't really going to change things between them—except physically. But they were both here for similar, if not identical, reasons, and if they happened to become closer, maybe they could work together even better.

She grabbed his hand and led him from the kitchen into the tiny hallway, and then flicked on her bedroom light as she pulled him through the door.

"Nice room," he said, glancing around. She tried to see it through his eyes. It was small, with one double bed in the middle, a narrow three-drawer dresser against the wall near the door, and a night table near the headboard. The furniture was serviceable, but not especially attractive. She hadn't spent any time or money decorating the place. There were no pictures on the walls, only a fluffy area rug beneath the bed on the wood floor. In short, it looked like the rest of this place—like a hotel suite where she was sleeping, eating and doing little else.

Which was fine with her. But was this room acceptable as a place for them to make love?

Apparently so, since without saying anything else Alan reached for her, pulled her flowing top over her head, then reached down to remove her slacks.

"Thanks," she said in response to his compliment about the room, even as she managed to start unbuttoning his shirt.

It didn't take long. In moments, they were both naked, standing there, staring at each other.

He was incredible. One hunky, sexy, muscular guy with an erection so long and thick that it invited her to reach for it. Caress it. Moan at the way it made her want him even more.

He didn't wait for her, though. His hands were stroking her, breasts first now that they were bare. And then he reached down and began stroking her most sensitive area.

She gasped, knowing she was growing wet. And hot. She wanted him. Right away.

But—

"Here," she said, taking his hand and leading him to the bed.

"Wait just a second." He bent down, reaching into his trousers for a small plastic package. Protection.

He must have been anticipating this, which was surprising. But it was a good thing. As attracted as she had been to him almost from the first, she really hadn't thought sex would be part of their quasi-business relationship. Or maybe carrying condoms was just something he did.

She wasn't about to ask.

When he rose again, she just looked at him, tearing her gaze from the very appealing and obvious part of him that all but beckoned her to the rest of him. He was tall, of course, and his muscular build suggested that he worked out a lot—not surprising for a government agent.

He was undoubtedly the sexiest man she had ever seen, and she wanted him, role-playing or reality or whatever.

"Alan," she whispered.

His smile was hot as his eyes roved down her body, as well. He reached out his hand, and she suddenly found herself lying beside him on the bed's beige coverlet.

She wanted to waste no time. She began by grasping his upper arm with one hand, kneading the hard muscles there. At the same time, she felt him reach out, touching her breasts once more, and then moving his hand down her front until it stopped at the hair covering her sex.

He shifted then, moving her legs apart as he began kissing her there, then using his tongue to taste and stroke her. She breathed heavily, irregularly, enjoying and focusing on the feeling for what seemed like a long time but was probably only seconds. And then she cried out, "Please, Alan."

He clearly heard what she wasn't saying. In moments, he'd pulled away, but only slightly. She wasn't sure where he had put the condom package, but it was back in his hand, and she saw and heard him rip it open.

"Let me," she said, attempting to smile.

"With pleasure," he rasped.

She took the condom. Before doing anything else, she bent and took his erection into her mouth, sucking it. And then she moved back enough to cover him with the sheath.

He moved on top of her then and was quickly and completely inside her, rocking gently back and forth at first and then pumping harder and harder until she reached completion, crying out and laughing at the same time even as he gasped, too.

He soon lay limply upon her, clearly spent, as she was.

His voice was ragged yet filled with humor as he said, "I think we'll be able to convince anyone, if we need to, that we're spending some time together because we've got some really fun kind of relationship."

Kelly was delighted that they spent even more time together that night. In that bedroom, and on that bed. In fact, Alan stayed until morning, and they engaged in two more bouts of incredible sex that took Kelly's breath away. And, finally, allowed her to sleep.

But Alan got up early and woke her, too. "Sorry, but I'd better head back to my place before showing up at work. But you can be sure I'll need breakfast, lunch or a snack at the Haven sometime today."

"With some of your coworkers so we can show off the way we look at each other now?" Kelly teased, although it really didn't feel that funny to her. Would they regard each other differently? Most likely. Or maybe it would be somewhat the same, but they wouldn't have to fake it as much.

"Maybe. Let's see how things go."

He had gotten out of bed then, headed for her small bathroom carrying his clothes and returned entirely dressed in the casual outfit she liked so much on him.

By then she had donned a knee-length green robe and was in the kitchen, making coffee in the small pot she kept there. "Want to sit down and join me?" She waved an empty mug at him.

"Just half a cup. I've got to be on my way." He looked great. Or maybe the enhanced smile he leveled on her just made her feel as if she were the happiest woman on earth.

As long as she didn't think of anything, anyone, beyond this room...

But Kelly figured Alan had been thinking about more than the wonderful night they had spent together as he sat down at the table, watching her at the counter, and started talking. "You should know that one of the reasons I'm heading back to my place is that I want to go over some of the secure files I have access to regarding you and your background—and Blue Haven. I was aware of the real estate connection to dissension between Stan Grodon and Andi, including about that property Jerome Baranka was promoting. Like I said, I'd met some of the town's other businesspeople who might contribute to Stan's campaign and all, and had checked on Baranka, but I hadn't previously run into him. I want to look in more detail at what we have on him, if anything, and also get some of the helpful research geeks who work for the Identity Division to check him out further, too."

"Really? That's wonderful." The coffee was ready, and Kelly poured Alan his half mug, then set it in front of him on the table. "But you know I mentioned him when I was being interviewed by the ID Division about what had been going on around here when my sister disappeared."

"Yes, I do know." Alan took a sip of coffee, smiled and took another, then continued. "As I said, I'd initially started out looking into the people Stan seemed to see often and even rely on. I was going to get to Baranka soon. Now I'll concentrate on him right away."

Kelly, who'd poured her own coffee and sat down across from Alan, leaned over the table toward him. "People Stan sees often and relies on? Have you checked out Paul Tirths yet?"

Alan's smile was grim. "Oh, yeah, and I acted damned friendly with the guy whenever I saw him, hoping to get him to talk. I know you told Judge Treena that Tirths had been the one to tell you what had happened to Andi, then retract it, so all you could claim was hearsay, not anyone's usable testimony."

"I've been watching for him, too." Kelly knew her voice was shaky and quiet.

"I met him when I first got here, but he's apparently on vacation or something right now. I gather he'll be back in a few days. But you'd better stay away from him to make sure your cover isn't blown."

"I know. I'm having to be so careful here...but it's worth it if I can do anything to help Eli. And..." She looked straight into Alan's eyes. "If I can *pretend*—" she trilled the word "—to be your girlfriend and use it as a backdoor way to see more of Stan, and—"

"Cool it." Alan laughed, took what looked like a

final sip and stood. "Time for me to go. But reminder—
please don't do or say anything to Stan, his minions
or anyone else that could blow what I'm doing here.
Got it?"

Kelly was standing by then, too, and she maneuvered her way around the table till she was up against
Alan. She felt her breasts tease his chest, even as his
erection started to grow against her. "Yes, sir." She
pulled his head down to give him a kiss.

It was another hot, enticing meeting of their lips and
tongues, and it tempted Kelly to march Alan right back
to her bedroom. But she didn't even try.

He stepped back first. "Remember that," he said.
"You called me 'sir' and at least pretended that you
consider me in charge. Well, I am in charge of this investigation, Kelly, so please remember that. You want
a positive resolution, and so do I—including ensuring
that Eli comes out of it okay. But this is what I know,
what I do. You're an amateur." His quick stare suggested she was an interloper, but it quickly eased into
something more persuasive. "Please listen and cooperate with me. Okay?"

She had been teasing when she'd said "Yes, sir." She
hadn't meant it to appear as if she considered Alan in
charge. Sure, what he said made sense. He had been
trained as a government operative.

But despite her wanting his opinion on approaches
and what to do, that didn't mean he was her command-
ing officer or anything like that. "I want to cooperate,"
she told him. "But please, let's talk often. Do things
together. All right?"

He didn't respond immediately, and his blank expression sent a pang of hurt through her.

"I'll see you later at the Haven," he said, then stepped forward, held her close again long enough to give her a brief kiss, then left her apartment.

What a night, Alan thought as he drove back to his own apartment. His body ached and felt sated at the same time.

And did he want more? Absolutely.

So if the people he dealt with here in Blue Haven assumed he had a relationship with Kelly, that was fine.

The problem was that he now did have a relationship with her. But he wasn't sure what it was.

Phenomenal sex, yes. Counterproductive task-related matters, also yes.

They shouldn't go together.

His place wasn't far from Kelly's, but it was certainly more homey—a larger, more personal place for him to live for the time being. He lived in a two-story triplex in a much bigger complex. He hadn't met many of his neighbors, but he hadn't needed to.

He had instead wanted to get to know everyone on or affiliated with city council to learn all he could about Stan Grodon.

Getting to know more of the town's businesspeople was also on his agenda if he couldn't find what he wanted soon, but he now wondered if it had been a mistake not to get to know Jerome Baranka.

Well, he would do so now.

He entered his place at ground level, then ran up the flight of steps to the small bedroom he used as an office. Instead of using the desktop computer, he unlocked a suitcase hidden under the desk and pulled out a laptop—one with software that was key for all CIU agents. He put it onto the desk beside the desktop's keyboard, booted up, then entered the current password—they changed frequently by a formula he knew well—to access the national resources it made available.

He looked up Baranka on the government site he liked best. It wasn't the first time he had sought information on that guy, but before he had just gotten a brief initial review of everyone whose names appeared in the Shereen Alsop file. And once he'd come here and settled in, he had gotten more detailed info on those he'd met, most especially the target of his assignment—Stan.

All his research had given him enough of a start to figure out who to focus on and spend the most time with here—other than Stan, since he didn't want the egotistical possible killer to feel threatened that a security guy was acting too friendly.

But he'd checked out others, including Councilwoman Arviss.

He hadn't mentioned that part to Kelly, because letting her know too many of the devices he relied on here wasn't a good idea.

The councilwoman appeared to be what she seemed, so allowing her to continue to work with, and champion, Eli Grodon should be fine.

He spent another ten minutes reviewing things and creating files to return to—never printing them, though, since they could wind up in the wrong hands.

Then he shut things down and headed to the floor below, where his bedroom was located. He showered first, then changed into a different suit for this day.

Would Kelly like this charcoal-gray one? He would see her at the Haven today, though he wasn't sure when.

He would definitely look forward to it, and to the non-act they would put on in front of other people.

Maybe he'd even find a way to get her alone and kiss her. To suggest a visit to his home sometime soon.

To—

Enough. He had a busy day awaiting him.

Chapter 11

Kelly had been at work at the Haven for nearly an hour. Contrary to how she normally felt, today she felt almost overdressed in her skimpy work outfit every time she thought of the night before, when she had been happily, enjoyably naked.

But she realized she was just laughing at herself.

"What's so funny?" Tobi asked. Kelly had just gone into the kitchen, which smelled like cinnamon, to place an order with the chefs, and Tobi was on her way out with a tray containing several delicious-looking omelets.

"Just having a good day." Kelly tried to tone down her grin. "How about you?"

The other server's pale hazel eyes scanned Kelly from head to toe. "I suspect you have reason to feel good," she said with a huge grin of her own. "I want to hear all about it later. Right now, I've got stuff to serve." Tobi walked briskly but carefully out the kitchen door.

Kelly watched her, swallowing hard. Was it that obvious what she had done last night? Or was Tobi just playing games with her, as she was sometimes prone to do?

If so, the timing appeared more than coincidental. Would everyone she knew somehow sense what she had been up to?

Just in case, she considered how to turn it off. She couldn't change into something less suggestive, but she could stop looking so happy, or—

"Did you bring an order in here?" Ella had just appeared in the kitchen near where the cooks were hard at work preparing breakfast dishes.

"I sure did." Kelly tried to sound pleasant without smiling at her boss, who was, as usual, wearing a stylish dress—a beige one today, with an orange print scarf around her neck. "The orders are for a table for six in my serving area, and they all seem hungry." Kelly started reciting some of the food they'd requested, some of the restaurant's best and priciest breakfast items.

Ella stopped her after a few seconds, waving her hands to cut her off. "That's good. Go give the order to the chefs. Don't just stand there."

"I—" Kelly stopped herself from saying anything. At least Ella hadn't said anything personal or suggestive— like that she could see Kelly looked especially happy, or satisfied, that morning.

Giving her boss a nod, she moved around her and presented the order to the cooks on the notepad she carried. She also gave them a verbal rundown.

"This all one order?" asked the lead chef.

"Yes."

"Check back in seven minutes."

Kelly hoped that was all it would take. In the meantime, she would go back to the table and serve the fruit juices, coffees and teas they had ordered.

As soon as she was out of the kitchen, she started looking around. Alan had said he would come here today sometime. Would he come for breakfast?

She felt her mouth begin to curl up into a smile, till she caught herself.

And in a few more seconds she knew that this wasn't a good time to smile at all.

Stan Grodon had walked in.

Of course he had. Kelly had already told herself many times that in this small town, she was likely to run into him often. Not only had he already shown up at the Haven several times since she had started working here, but she had seen him other places, too. That was a good thing...maybe. Unless he recognized her.

But until she figured out a way to get Eli alone and learn what he was experiencing without acting inappropriately toward him, she had to make use of all advantages she could. So far, all she'd managed was frustration at how little she had seen her nephew, and her inability to do anything positive for him.

If seeing Stan around here got her even a tiny lead on hard evidence against him to turn over to Alan, that would be great. It could even ultimately result in her making things better for Eli. But what was the likelihood of that?

This time the grin she pasted on her face was false. Since she was the closest server to Stan and the three other people he'd brought in, and Ella was still in the kitchen, Kelly was the one to say, "Please have a seat anywhere you'd like."

His back was toward the other guests he'd led in. Kelly recognized one of them, the woman. She'd been with him at Tony's Lounge the other night, his apparent date. Now, though, she was dressed professionally in a suit, so maybe he knew her from city council.

"I'd like a seat where you'll be our server," he responded softly, aiming a huge, suggestive leer at her.

She nearly gagged, wishing she could say that all the tables she took care of were filled, but the Haven's dining area was far from full.

And if he was dating that woman, he had a lot of nerve flirting with someone else while he was with her. But Kelly already knew that Stan had a lot of nerve.

If she showed the group to one of Lang's tables, would that be okay? Ella seemed in no worse of a grumpy mood than usual, but that didn't mean she wouldn't fire Kelly if she embarrassed her in front of a government official, even by doing something minor.

Besides, avoiding Stan wouldn't get Kelly what she ultimately wanted. She needed to face him head-on wherever possible, no matter how much he acted as the lowlife he was, as long as she didn't give herself away.

And as long as it helped, but didn't hurt, Eli.

"Then by all means, please sit at this table." Kelly drew closer and waved her hand toward one in the area where she'd been assigned.

"Thank you, gorgeous." Stan's leer disappeared as he turned and gestured to where he wanted those accompanying him to sit.

Okay, she could play this role. She looked down,

pretending to blush. Would that embarrass him in front of the people he was with? She doubted it. And at the moment, they all were paying attention to Stan, not her.

She took a moment to assess them. The other two, likewise dressed in suits, were also men. Did any of them, including the woman, work for the city? Kelly hadn't seen them at the lunch she had helped to cater.

Or, like Jerome Baranka, were they businesspeople who wanted something from Stan—and were perhaps willing to pay for it?

Kelly would try to eavesdrop. Maybe something she overheard would be useful to Alan. And she wouldn't be above using anything she heard to help Eli, if she could determine how.

She began to take their drink orders, which were mostly coffees and waters for now. Stan stuck with the former. "What do you want, Dora?" he asked the woman at his left. So she was Dora. Dora ordered tea.

"I'll be right back with them," Kelly said, feeling a little bummed when Stan didn't even look at her now. His eyes were on the menu. And when she returned with the drinks, he was involved in a conversation with the man to his right, a good-looking guy with a dark complexion, thinning hair and an amused gaze that he watched Stan with.

Which of them wanted something from the other?

She purposely interrupted them. "What can I get everyone?"

An omelet for Stan and for one of the men, pancakes for the other guy, and scrambled eggs for Dora.

Stan barely glanced toward Kelly as he ordered. Damn. She was possibly losing an opportunity, but how could she take advantage of it? Swallow her disgust and make herself flirt with him? But if that annoyed Dora, Stan might retaliate. He'd done an adequate job so far of hiding his flirtation from that woman.

Too bad Alan wasn't here. Maybe they could come up with something together. That was their cover, as well as reality. They were *together*, in more ways than one.

Ready to turn in their order, Kelly sighed and started walking to the kitchen. Tobi joined her. "Everything okay with you?" she asked.

Kelly realized she must not look nearly as good as she had when she'd first arrived. She certainly didn't feel as good.

"Of course. I'm serving at least one big shot from the city. Are there any others here today?"

"You mean our illustrious City Councilman Grodon? I know you've waited on him before, but I'd suggest being especially nice to him. He can be a great tipper." Tobi lifted her eyebrows as she smiled and waved, then hurried in a different direction.

Stan wasn't likely to come up with the main tips she wanted from him here, Kelly thought. She couldn't exactly bring up Andi, or even Eli, without causing a problem.

But she could play her role. First, she turned in the order, then delivered food to a table next to Stan's. She pivoted to look at him from there. "Your food will be ready shortly. Anything you need in the meantime?" She knew what she said could be taken suggestively, especially by this man.

He glanced toward his left, where Dora was talking to the guy on her other side. Then Stan looked up at Kelly, let his eyes roll down her scantily clad body and said, completely in character, "Oh, yes." But instead of saying anything suggestive or disgusting he just said, "Some more water, please."

"Of course." Kelly wished she could read his mind, and not only about his relationship with Dora. Of course, Kelly had wanted to do that a lot when she'd been in Stan's presence before, ever since her sister disappeared.

Prior to her—Shereen—leaving town, she had figured that sometimes what he was thinking about was the best way to get rid of her. Permanently. He'd even tried it a few times.

She brought more water and iced tea, taking her time refilling their glasses and listening to their conversations.

Stan was again talking to the guy beside him, saying how much opportunity there was to start new businesses in Blue Haven, even to expand existing businesses with offices or new retail outlets here. And additional restaurants, even better than this one. There'd be competition, sure, but there was always room for more. Had the guy ever seen the Blue View? That was an expensive but utterly delightful restaurant on top of a cliff overlooking the cove in the Pacific that gave Blue Haven its name.

That gave her a pretty good idea of what Stan was up to now, and if she didn't already know what a horrible person he was, she might consider him an asset to this city, trying to attract more business and more revenue.

But his eating here today was turning out to be worthless to her.

She was soon able to deliver the table's meals. They assured her there wasn't anything else they needed just then. But the old Stan was still lurking inside. Kelly felt a pinch on her behind as she turned to go. When she looked back, all four people at the table had started to eat—though Stan turned his head slightly toward her after looking at the others and gave her a quick wink.

Damn him! She wanted to slug him. But she couldn't. Wouldn't. That wouldn't get him to talk to her or anyone else.

Although...sex last night with Alan probably put the idea into her head, but what if she was more seductive around Stan when there weren't other people close by, even when he didn't initiate it? The idea made her feel ill inside, but she wouldn't have to go through with anything.

Maybe she could get him to start talking. Bragging about past conquests...like his wife.

That would put her much too close to him, though. She'd be more at risk that he would recognize her. No, she couldn't do that.

So how could a mere family restaurant server get to know him—and, more important, his son—beyond just seeing him here?

As full of questions and anger as Kelly was, she made herself concentrate on waiting on other customers in her serving area with all the friendliness and grace that Ella expected of her.

When she glanced back at that table, Stan seemed right at home talking to all of them, but he seemed to mostly pay attention to Dora. Who was she? Did she work for the city or someone else? Or have her own business?

Were she and Stan a couple?

If they were dating, maybe the woman also knew

Eli. Maybe she would wind up being Kelly's key to seeing more of him.

Kelly knew she needed to learn more, talk to Dora to determine if she could be of any use. But how?

Maybe she could run her thoughts by Alan. He was coming here sometime today.

Stan soon indicated they were finished, and Kelly brought him the check. He gave her his credit card, and when the transaction was completed she realized that Tobi was right. Stan tipped well.

Maybe to encourage her to get to know him better. It was exactly what she wanted, but not the way he undoubtedly had in mind.

After watching Stan and company maneuver between the tables and out the door, Kelly decided this might be a good time to text Alan and ask about his plans—but it turned out she didn't need to. He entered the Haven almost the moment the others had left.

He saw her immediately and waved. Without glancing around to see who might notice, Kelly waved back and motioned him to come over. The place was filling up, but she would definitely find him a table.

She'd also figure out a means and location where they could talk.

Talk business, of course—including her latest thoughts about Stan.

But as Alan drew closer, a huge sexy grin on his handsome face, she acknowledged that there were reasons other than business that she was delighted to see Alan.

There she was. It was all Alan could do to keep himself from wending his way among the restaurant's tables, taking that beautiful, sexy woman into his arms and giving her one heck of a big kiss.

To play their game, of course. Act out their roles. But also because he figured she might need a little warmth after having had her nemesis in here again: Stan.

Alan had seen the councilman on his way out with some of the town's business folks that he recognized, but not the one he now especially wanted to meet and talk with: Jerome Baranka. But he would watch out for Baranka and find a way to talk to him somehow, whether Stan was around or not.

He hadn't stood there more than a few seconds when Kelly clearly noticed him, too, and approached with her arms not exactly extended in welcome, but her hands facing him as if she had an urge to hug him, as well.

"Can't stay long," he said when she caught up with him between tables near the door. "Just had a few minutes off and wanted to grab a cup of coffee."

"Please come in," she said, and within moments he wanted to stroke her soft cheeks, pull her close. If he read the almost pleading expression on her lovely face correctly, she had something on her mind.

But before they got close to each other, she looked over his shoulder, then maneuvered around him beside a table where two men were eating and motioned for someone to walk toward her. Alan turned and saw two mothers, each holding the hand of a young boy. "Let's get you a good spot and some high chairs," Kelly said to them, then shot an apologetic glance his way.

"Let me help," he said.

Kelly's expression looked both amused and grateful. In a few minutes, those two families were seated at a table near the door—probably not one where Kelly served, but when her boss, Ella, hurried over to check things out, she seemed happy with Kelly.

"You deserve a quick break," Ella said to her, letting her inquisitive gaze move between them.

"Oh, thank you," Kelly said, then looked at her boss. "I know it's against one of your rules, but would you mind if I grabbed a cup of coffee here with Alan? I'll be glad to serve us and stay out of everyone's way."

"And I'll pay," Alan said, "and give Kelly a nice tip."

"I would hope so." Ella's hazel eyes gleamed as her gaze again moved from one to the other. She was a pretty woman, maybe in her forties, but from what Alan had noted about her, she ruled her employees here with an iron fist—or maybe a heavy frying pan. But apparently she could be nice to them after all.

Like now.

It was a good thing, too. As Ella apparently went to tell the other servers to cover for her, Kelly motioned him to follow her among the river of tables till they reached an empty one in the corner near the hallway to the restrooms and offices. He helped her into a chair and took the one opposite her.

He liked how her luminous brown eyes shone and her smile lit up her entire face. "This, I gather, is unheard of," she said quietly. "I want to find out what caused Ella to act so nice today. But right now I'd better go get us some coffee. Regular, with cream, correct?"

"Correct." He watched her lithesome body in her skimpy uniform as she rose, wanting again to touch her, but not here. "Then we'll talk."

Chapter 12

Kelly did her thing as super server, especially now that the person she was serving was Alan. She didn't need to impress anyone but him.

Well, maybe Ella, since she still didn't know why her boss was being so nice. Maybe she'd figure that out later.

Now, after strutting just a little sexily since it was Alan and not Stan she approached, she set a mug of steaming black coffee down on the table before him, put her own down, too, then handed the metal cream container to Alan. He looked at her with an expression she read as thanks...and more. He seemed amused. And, well, was the lust in the air only because she felt that way about him, or was it reciprocal? Or was he merely performing here, in keeping with the way they'd decided to play things?

All of the above, she figured.

He waved toward her seat with his right hand—one of his strong, sexy hands that had been all over her last night...

She felt herself start to flush, and after taking her seat, she sipped her coffee to give herself an excuse to feel, and look, so warm.

"Can't stay long," Alan warned, "but I'm here because I promised to come."

"Big doings at Government Plaza?" she asked.

"Meetings, meetings and more meetings this afternoon." He leaned toward her. "I'm not sure what the discussions will be about, but all city council members will be involved."

What he didn't say, but told her anyway, was that Councilwoman Arviss would be busy—too busy to have her son and Eli in to stuff envelopes today.

That was okay. Kelly couldn't keep showing up every time they were there anyway, as much as she wanted to.

"I get it." She looked around. There was a family occupying a table behind Alan, but otherwise she had chosen an area that wasn't too busy. She could talk here as long as she kept her voice low. "Did you happen to see the people accompanying...you-know-who when he left?"

He nodded. "I recognized them. Local business folk who sometimes come to meetings, mostly about promoting Blue Haven and boosting tourism and spending money, that kind of thing. Without raising taxes, of course. But they didn't include..."

He tapered off, choosing to be ambiguous, too. Good. They were on the same wavelength. She figured he referred to the real estate guy, Baranka.

But she had to get a little more specific now. "One of them—well, we saw Councilman Grodon out in a more social atmosphere the other night."

Alan would know what she was talking about—when they had run into Stan and the woman she had just learned was named Dora at Tony's Lounge. He nodded.

"I... I'm impressed by her and would like to meet her."

"Why?" he asked.

Kelly didn't feel comfortable talking about it here. "No big deal." She looked so intensely into his brown eyes that he undoubtedly knew she was lying. "We can discuss it all later." She paused. "Can we meet for dinner tonight?"

"Sounds good to me." Alan's grin looked genuine. "We'll talk later and make plans."

He left about five minutes later after finishing only one mug of coffee, paying for it and Kelly's, too—and, yes, leaving Kelly a generous tip. For show, she figured, since Ella, who handled the bill at the cash register and ran his credit card through, including the tip, appeared impressed.

Kelly had just taken the orders of three college-aged kids at a table near the door when Ella approached her and told her how much the tip was.

"Not bad," Kelly responded, smiling. "Thanks for letting me take that break."

"I gather you've got something going with that security guy." The usual intense expression Ella leveled on her staff was there, but it was tempered with a small inquisitive grin that lit up her attractive face.

"I...well, I don't really know yet, but I wouldn't

mind if we got to know each other better." Would Ella consider that a good thing? At least it wasn't grounds for her to fire Kelly.

"Well, I know he's started ordering food from here, including for events for the bigwigs at Government Plaza. If you can encourage more of that, I'll let you have more breaks when he comes in."

"Of course." Kelly felt herself sigh a bit in relief. There was an explanation. Whether she could deliver on Ella's hopes—whether Alan could deliver— remained to be seen.

Ella headed toward the door, and Tobi approached from her nearby serving area. "So when are you going to tell me what's going on—with that guy, and with Ella, and—"

"With everything, right?" Lang had also joined them.

"It's too soon to know" was all Kelly let herself say. She liked her fellow workers here—a lot. But telling them anything, even that she really was interested in Alan the security guy, seemed like too much information, at least for now.

She only hoped she would soon accomplish all she had set out to do here, and assist Alan in his success, too.

Then, when Stan was somehow stopped, she would be thrilled to shout it all to the world.

Including her new friends here.

On his brief walk back to Government Plaza, Alan called Judge Treena on his specially encrypted and secure phone, but she wasn't available. Instead, he spoke with his immediate superior officer at the CIU, Director Walt Jones, who reported to Judge Treena.

"Nothing new," he told Walt, a sixtysomething former army colonel who had been in government security for over fifteen years. "As I told Judge Treena before, I am in contact with our missing subject and keeping an eye on her. At the moment, she's not in my way and hasn't been recognized, so I wouldn't suggest you send a team to extract her. She might actually be an asset to my assignment."

"You know that's against policy," Walt stated.

"I do, but I also know this isn't the first time this protocol has been used."

"Interesting. You after a new main squeeze as well as a collaborator?"

"I only want it to look that way to people here so our collaboration will go more smoothly." No way would he tell his superior, or anyone else associated with the Identity Division, that he actually felt attracted to Kelly.

Besides, unlike the other situation they alluded to, there was no way he'd wind up getting that close to Kelly. He'd do his job here, she'd help because it might wind up fixing things for her nephew, and when they were done with that they'd be done with everything else, as well.

"Well, all right, though you know I'll discuss this with Judge Treena. If she says otherwise, you'll need to deal with it."

"Understood." Alan said goodbye and hung up.

He did understand. Whether he would comply was another matter—and he found this realization disturbing. He was all about obeying orders. That came from experience.

He was now on the sidewalk a block away from the plaza. His thoughts roiled from the recollection.

It had been years since he had been a navy SEAL. He'd joined the military right after college and excelled there as he always had in school. He'd attributed his success to getting along with people—and following orders, especially in the navy.

But on one mission in the Middle East, nearly his last, when he and his team were given orders to avoid attacking an enemy despite a clear threat to civilians on a fishing boat, he saw a fellow officer choose to attack—but the enemy force was prepared. The fellow officer came out of it okay, and so did the fishermen, but another man on that mission was shot and nearly killed.

Though he could understand why the officer who chose to disobey had done so, the incident reinforced Alan's determination to follow orders, and to despise those who refused to.

Which made his camaraderie with Kelly especially difficult, despite the good reason for it.

Alan noticed now that he was surrounded by people outside the government building. Many headed up the steps while others exited. The building was tall, a faux marble, and fairly regal-looking for a town this small, although it was the West Coast and relatively upscale. It would be a nice location to grow up in, maybe, as Kelly's alter ego had done.

He hurried upstairs with the crowd and headed to the security office on the first floor to check in. None of his colleagues were there, which didn't surprise him.

They'd be up on the fourth floor, preparing to observe the proceedings in the council meeting room and its environs that afternoon. Alan headed there as well.

The hallway was full of people, and not only city council members and their assistants. Some were people Alan had seen with Stan recently, businesspeople he apparently was friendly with for whatever reason—although Alan suspected it was mostly for Stan's own financial interests. Maybe these people were simply generous with their donations and campaign contributions, but Alan wouldn't be surprised if more than one was engaging in bribery.

The group all seemed headed for the meeting room. Seeing Dodd down the hall also observing gave Alan some relief. From a security perspective, things appeared under control.

As the hallway emptied more, Alan saw Councilwoman Regina Joralli exit from her office near where Dodd stood. The all-business president of the council immediately placed herself in the middle of the remaining group and made her way to the front of the line to enter the meeting room.

Then Stan emerged from his office, and he wasn't alone. The woman with him was the same one who'd been with him and others earlier when they'd left the Haven—also the same woman who had been with him at Tony's Lounge the other night.

The woman Kelly had expressed an interest in getting to know better in case she happened to be Stan's current main squeeze. What was her name?

Dora something, wasn't it?

It now looked as if this afternoon's meetings might present opportunities Alan hadn't anticipated.

He felt antsy waiting for the rest of those in the hallway to file into the meeting room, and was glad when he could finally follow.

The room was crowded, but all council members were seated around the table in the middle. So were some visitors, including Dora, who unsurprisingly sat beside Stan.

Would Alan get an opportunity to speak with her to get more info on who she was, so that he would have more than her first name and the town of Blue Haven to plug into his secure data sites?

As it turned out, he learned a lot more just standing there keeping an eye—and ear—on things than he'd anticipated.

And wouldn't Kelly be surprised?

This felt like a real date.

Alan had picked Kelly up at her apartment a few minutes ago, after she returned from work, showered and changed into one of the few pretty dresses she had brought along. It was silky and pale blue, with short sleeves and a slim, knee-length skirt.

"So we're going to the Blue View?" she asked. Previously, both over the phone and when he had insisted on coming upstairs to get her, Alan had seemed in a strange mood, as if he had information he was happy about but wasn't sharing.

Well, maybe she would learn what it was.

"Yes, we are." Alan glanced toward her briefly as he drove his gray SUV through Blue Haven in the direction of the cliffs holding the elite restaurant.

Alan hadn't been near Kelly when she'd overheard Stan talking to the business guy beside him at the

Haven, asking if he had ever been to the Blue View. Even so, were they headed there because Alan had reason to believe Stan was there, perhaps with the man he'd been chatting with?

But her goal wasn't to follow Stan around—unless he was taking his son out to dinner at that expensive restaurant, which Kelly doubted, at least not without some ulterior motive.

"Sounds good to me," she said, contemplating how to find out what Alan was really up to. "Is this just to give more credence to our acting like a couple here? Do you think some of Stan's cronies will be there? Even if they see us there, that doesn't necessarily mean they'll look at us as anything but a security guy trying to impress a restaurant server, so they're unlikely to open up and answer questions about their businesses or their relationships with Stan."

"You're right, but I learned something today that will potentially make this dinner particularly enjoyable. And even if nothing comes to pass on that front, we should still have a good time. Oh, and in case you're wondering, I'm paying. A security guy may not make a lot of money, but he earns more than a waitress, and besides, this security guy wants to be seen as someone trying hard to impress the server of his dreams."

The grin he shot at Kelly was cute and sexy and made her feel all warm inside—as if what he was saying were real. But of course she knew better.

She smiled nevertheless. "Thank you, sir. I'll definitely be impressed."

"That's good. Any idea what kind of food they serve there?"

"I know what they used to serve, but let me check."

Kelly looked up the menu on her phone, and they discussed the possibilities as Kelly refused to gulp or comment on the high prices. Alan clearly knew what he was getting into.

They quickly passed through the streets of downtown, and Alan started up the narrow, winding road that led up the nearby mountain toward the developed cliff-side area containing the Blue View. Kelly hadn't been there since returning to this town. She hadn't gone there often before, either. There were a few expensive shops near the restaurant and a resort hotel, but not much else there, and Shereen's budget as a schoolteacher hadn't allowed for too many visits to that exclusive area.

Twilight approached, but fortunately streetlights lined the road. They met a few cars coming down the hill, and Alan caught up with a short line of vehicles heading the same direction. The road circled the mountain somewhat, and from some angles the skyline meeting the ocean was visible and breathtaking.

Eventually, they reached the restaurant, where the side of the mountain had been carved into a large, flat area where businesses were located. Alan parked the car, then, as Kelly opened her door, went around to help her out of the passenger seat.

A perfect gentleman, Kelly thought. Or at least that was the impression he wanted to give—not that he had to do anything like that around her, and she doubted anyone else was paying attention, though she noticed a few other patrons getting in or out of cars around them.

"In case you're wondering, I made a reservation," Alan said as they strode through the parking lot and up to the front door of the restaurant.

"Great idea."

The Blue View looked chalet-like despite the fact that this area in Southern California got no snow. It was one story high, had several angled slopes to its roof and appeared to be constructed out of reddish wood. Its walls were filled with huge windows, and in the dim light Kelly could see the tall ceiling inside as well as some tables.

"Nice place," Alan remarked as they entered through the wide door.

"Sure is," Kelly agreed, looking around. It was much as she remembered from the very few times she had been here before—quaint and elegant and filled with people dressed for the occasion.

The seats half circling the entrance were filled, apparently with people waiting for tables. There was a tall wooden stand nearby with a clipboard on it that must be used by the maître d', although he wasn't there at the moment.

But soon someone approached the stand—a hostess, not a maître d'.

A familiar-looking hostess.

Really? Stan Grodon was flirting with a mere restaurant hostess? Or was there more to the story than that?

For the person who approached was none other than Dora, Stan's date the other night and the woman who had been with him at the Haven that day.

Kelly glanced at Alan in amazement.

Before he stepped forward to give his name to the woman greeting them, he shot a glance toward Kelly... and grinned.

Chapter 13

Alan hadn't intended this moment to be a test of Kelly's sharpness and ingenuity...or maybe he had for reasons even he considered inappropriate right now. She was smart. She had motives of her own. But they were working together now, no matter what she had done to get here.

He could have—should have—warned her whom he felt fairly sure they'd run into here, since Dora had indicated she would be at the Blue View tonight at the time of the reservation Alan had asked her to make for him.

The look Kelly shot him now appeared both justifiably puzzled and angry. But she turned her head immediately and looked at Dora as he stepped forward to confirm their reservation.

"Of course, Alan," Dora responded warmly. "So glad you came." She wore a nice tailored dress, nothing like the sexy, sparse outfit they had seen her in with Stan at Tony's Lounge, nor the professional business suit she had worn that day at Government Plaza. No matter what she wore, she was one attractive lady, which undoubtedly was a major factor in Stan's apparent interest in her.

But since Alan had learned earlier that day that her parents, the Shallners, had bought the Blue View Restaurant a few months ago and she was instrumental in helping them run it, he had no doubt that her family's money was another reason for Stan's interest.

Kelly had mentioned a desire to befriend Dora. They hadn't discussed exactly why yet, but he suspected she wanted to learn what Dora knew about Stan—and maybe, Eli. Alan thought it was a potentially good idea.

In fact, the situation could work out really well since these two women were both in hospitality and both worked at restaurants—notwithstanding the major differences in the nature of those eateries and their connections with them. If some camaraderie developed between them, Kelly might be able to learn something useful from this woman in whom Stan Grodon appeared to be interested.

Now, once he and Kelly were seated and had a modicum of privacy, Alan would explain this to her and help her come up with a way to start chatting with their hostess.

If it made sense, he might even apologize.

It turned out he didn't need to explain anything. As Dora picked up a couple of large menus from the stand and encouraged them to follow her, Kelly inserted herself in front of Alan and beside the other woman. "This place is so wonderful," she gushed. "It's my first time here. I've only been in Blue Haven a short while, and I'm a server at the Haven Restaurant. I really like it there, but it must be amazing to work at a place like this."

Of course Kelly wouldn't know that Dora was part of the family that owned this place and might somehow embarrass herself. But he could step in and interrupt if things seemed to be going south.

For now, Dora just turned toward Kelly. She was shorter than Kelly and had to look up through her clearly false eyelashes. Her hair was a pale blond that also didn't look real, and she gave the impression of being a model, or at least having a model's grace and looks.

Some of that could be said for Kelly, too, at least partly thanks to the new look she had been given by the Identity Division, complete with darker, wavier hair and different contours to her attractive face and body than she'd had before she'd had her identity changed, been put on a diet and exercise regimen despite not being overweight to begin with, and taught model-like comportment. Alan had seen Shereen's before photos when he was given the undercover assignment here to gather evidence to support Shereen's claims against the apparent murderer of her sister.

"My family owns a restaurant in LA," Dora was saying now.

Alan had a difficult time hearing her as he walked behind them, but the crowd noise here wasn't as loud or boisterous as at the Haven, and he suspected the wall paneling improved the acoustics—it was undoubtedly expensive.

"But my parents decided to expand our interests,"

Dora continued, "and learned that this place was for sale. They jumped on it, and I was delighted to take over managing it for them."

As far as Alan could tell, she was doing a good job. Even if she wasn't, she might have access to her family's money.

"That's so cool," Kelly said. "You know, I'd really like to get together and talk to you about it. I love my job at the Haven, and working right in downtown Blue Haven is wonderful. But this place is so outstanding. I realize you might not be looking for new servers or, even if you're open to the idea, I might not be your ideal candidate, but I'd like to at least discuss it with you."

They had maneuvered around rows of tables covered in attractive white cloths, many with decorative carafes of wine in the center and nearly all occupied by richly dressed patrons. They had just reached a table near one of the vast windows overlooking not the ocean but the parking lot. Under other circumstances Alan might have requested a different one, but he didn't want to undermine what Kelly was up to, so this would be fine.

Besides, he suspected they would be back here again soon, maybe often, at least until Kelly had sucked all the information she could out of Dora.

"We're always open to finding more good help," Dora said as Alan pulled the chair out for Kelly. "We're not looking for anyone at the moment, but maybe soon. In any event, I'd be glad to talk with you about your experience and whether you could fulfill our needs."

"That would be so wonderful!" Alan was amused by Kelly's assumed gushing personality. "Soon? Maybe tomorrow morning? I have Sundays off."

"How about around ten?" Dora asked. "Things are generally manageable here at that time on Sundays."

"I'll be here." Kelly's smile was huge, and she looked excited. This could lead to fulfillment of her goal, Alan realized, so why not? Dora knew Stan and might have some useful knowledge about him.

On the other hand—well, Kelly would need to be careful and discreet in the way she asked.

Somehow, he had a feeling she would do just fine.

"Why?" Kelly demanded quietly once Dora had handed them their menus, told them to enjoy their meals and headed back toward the front of the restaurant.

"Why what?" Alan asked.

"I assume you knew Dora would be here, but you didn't tell me. Why?"

She had an idea, though. It was a test of sorts. How would she handle herself in a situation like that, surprised yet needing to play it correctly or blow a potentially good source of information?

Before he answered, she went on. "What would you have done if I'd made a scene, tried to pounce on Dora here to get any insight she might have on Eli? You could have prepared me."

Alan just smiled, damn him. "I'd have taken over if you started to blow it. But I knew you'd figure things out and handle them right. I kind of thought of it as a game as well as a test, and you won."

Was that a glimmer of pride that she saw in the way he drew the ends of his lips up into a sexy smile? He spoke softly, too, but fortunately, even though this place wasn't nearly as noisy as the Haven, there were enough people talking around them to cover what they were saying.

A very pleasant female server came over just then, much more professionally clad than Kelly at the Haven in a black dress with a belt at the waist, dark stockings and black shoes with low heels. Kelly regarded her with a touch of envy, but only for a moment. It was time to order their drinks.

Kelly shot a snide grin toward Alan. She had only glanced at the drink menu, but she knew what she wanted: a glass of champagne. Expensive champagne.

After all, she was now celebrating. Whatever the reason for Alan's test, she had passed and then some.

She had proved she could be flexible. Rise to any occasion.

But somehow she just prayed that what she was doing—what they were doing—would have results soon. Very soon.

What would Dora tell her about Eli tomorrow? Anything at all? And if not, surely she could reveal something about Stan. Kelly could hardly wait.

For now, though, that champagne sounded wonderful. Alan ordered some, too, and shortly they were toasting each other.

That was fine for now. But Kelly couldn't wait until they were able to toast their success in bringing Stan down, avenging Andi and saving Eli.

Their meal was great. Alan ordered salmon, and Kelly ordered a mixed seafood salad. They didn't talk any more about Dora or their plot to get the answers they both sought. Instead, they discussed portions of his work that he could talk about in public, places where he had lived—mostly East Coast, around the DC area, and places in California where it would be fun to sightsee, many of which he figured Kelly had seen…before.

Kelly smiled each time Dora passed by to show other patrons to their seats. Alan wished he could be in on their conversation tomorrow, but that wouldn't make sense.

He would discuss questions for Kelly to ask on their way home later.

Their server came by a few times to ask if all was well—and to pour more champagne. They took their time, but eventually they were done eating.

When the server brought their check, Alan gulped and made a face as if horrified by the amount, then he grinned. "It's okay. I asked for it with my attitude before. And you earned this meal and more."

Was he mistaken, or was Kelly's return smile suggestive? It sure looked that way, and he was glad he was still seated when his body started to react.

He handed over his credit card. Once he'd gotten the receipt and added a generous tip, he stood and approached Kelly to pull out her chair for her. Gentlemanliness was certainly called for in a place like this. But she didn't wait. Instead, she took a few steps away from him quickly, as if to show who was in charge. She maneuvered along an aisle between tables until she reached one of the wide windows that looked out over the ocean. He joined her. It was dark outside so the water wasn't really visible, except for some reflections of light from above, but the view still added to this place's character. He put his arm around her briefly for show, enjoying the feel of her against him.

On their way out she stopped to talk to Dora at the reception stand, thanking her and saying she looked forward to seeing her the next day.

Kelly was a trouper, Alan thought. She was doing everything right. He could have ruined this evening for both of them by embarrassing her, but she came out on top.

And the idea of her being on top...well, that generated some especially hot ideas—not that any would necessarily come to fruition, darn it. Not tonight, at least, since any interest that Kelly might have shown was probably payback for his earlier attitude. She would simply say no now.

Wouldn't she?

He drove slowly on the way back down the mountain, despite how well the streetlights illuminated the road. They discussed her approach the next day for extracting any information Dora happened to have about Stan—and Eli.

"Just stay fascinated about this town and its people and places, and make your inquiries subtle but enthusiastic," Alan advised.

"Yes, sir." From the corner of his eye, he saw her give a not-very-professional salute. "Don't worry. I'll do fine."

He felt certain she would.

When he pulled up in front of her apartment building, he found a parking spot on the street. As a security guy, he had an urge to walk her upstairs. Additional urges, too. But maybe she wouldn't want anything like that—

"Would you like to come upstairs with me?" she

asked in a husky voice. She still sat in the passenger seat, and he saw her eyelids lower in a fully sensual gaze.

"Yes," he said. "I would."

Was this going to become a habit? Had it already?

The day had been busy enough that last night seemed a long time ago, at least in some ways. But inviting Alan to join her upstairs brought it all back to her.

Was this a bad idea? He'd played her a bit today, even tested her, and now they walked briskly up the wide, steep steps to her apartment, with her leading the way as if she was eager to get him up there.

Which, if she was truthful to herself, she was. It was part of their ruse to the rest of Blue Haven, after all.

And if that was the only reason, she could also pretend she hadn't done anything contrary to the Identity Division's orders.

At her floor, she stepped into the hallway feeling more out of breath than usual after that short trek. It had to be anticipation causing her respiration to increase and grow irregular.

Alan was beside her in an instant, and she hurried past the first door until she arrived at her own apartment, reaching into her purse for her key.

In moments, they were inside her small living room. Alan closed the door behind him.

"Would you like me to make us some coffee?" She tried to keep her breathing normal.

"Here's what I'd like."

She was suddenly in Alan's strong arms as he pulled her close against his hard body. His mouth came down on hers and robbed her of any further breathing, at least for a moment. She threw herself into that kiss, hugging him tightly to her, teasing him just a little with her tongue until his responded by entering her mouth with quick, sensual thrusts resembling sex.

She suddenly couldn't wait, wanted it immediately. "Let's go—" she tried to say against him, but didn't need to speak any further.

He didn't let go of her, though, but held her tightly to him as they hurried down the short hallway to her bedroom.

A while later, Alan lay beside Kelly, pleased and sated and feeling as if this was exactly where he wanted to be.

He exorcised any feelings of guilt—again. At least for now.

"Are you staying the night?"

He liked how her tone was soft and throaty, suggestive and inviting. He wanted to say—no, shout—yes.

But although he had remained here the night before when they had first engaged in such mind-blowing sex, he couldn't just move in here or even pretend to. He had a conference call scheduled with the ID Division early in the morning. Since it was Sunday, he only had to walk through Government Plaza, which should be pretty much unoccupied, a couple of times on patrol for his cover job. And he definitely wasn't going to get on the phone here.

Sure, he could stay for a while…but he knew exactly where that would lead. He needed some sleep tonight, and so did Kelly. She would need to be awake and alert, too, for her get-together with Dora.

"I appreciate the invitation," he finally said, not

sure whether it had in fact been an invitation or just an inquiry, "but I'd better get back to my place. I've got some things scheduled tomorrow, and so do you."

He turned onto his side to look at her. She, too, was on her side, and remained on top of the covers, as well. She was still bare, and he had an urge to reach over, capture one of her breasts in his hand and begin playing once more.

But he didn't.

"True," she said softly. And then she sat up and rolled off the bed. Her back to him, she reached into the nearby small closet and pulled out a robe, which she used to immediately cover herself. "So would you like some coffee now?" Her tone had become almost normal, no hint of what they'd done, what she had sort of invited him to do again.

"No, thanks," he said. "I'd better just get on my way. But maybe we can get together again soon."

"I'd like that," Kelly said. She walked him to the door, and after a final good-night kiss, Alan found himself smiling as he left.

Chapter 14

She felt relaxed. She felt wonderful.

But Kelly still did not fall asleep easily that night.

She lay in bed mostly on her side, her head resting on the softness of two pillows, her comfy pajamas on over her still-sensitive flesh.

No, she wasn't sleeping alone in the nude. But she couldn't help thinking about and rehashing her latest sexual encounter with Alan. Wondering what it would have been like had he decided to stay the night.

And when she forced her thoughts off that delightful musing that simply wasn't to be, it segued over to the other very different matter engaging her mind, as always these days: Eli.

How would she handle her meeting with Dora the next morning? She had a lot of ideas of questions to ask regarding Stan, Dora's relationship with him, and what she knew about him and his home life, such as it was. But could Kelly be subtle enough to drive the conversation there without arousing Dora's curiosity?

Was young Eli asleep now, comfortable in his own bed?

Was he safe?

How was his father treating him at this moment?

Kelly hadn't had to think long and hard about coming here to help Eli when she'd realized long-distance that he was in trouble. She'd just done it. But now that she was here, she'd hardly seen him, hardly spoken with him—and hadn't yet learned enough about his current status and what she could do to help him.

She hadn't been back in Blue Haven long, but it was beginning to feel like an eternity—at least regarding her sweet nephew.

And how could she help to get his horrible father away from him?

She'd been allowing herself the distraction of Alan, not that she could avoid it, or wanted to.

But maybe, just maybe, she'd be able to find another path tomorrow toward accomplishing what she had come here for.

Fortunately, although Alan did not sleep long that night, it was a deep enough sleep to allow him to wake feeling somewhat refreshed despite the early hour— five thirty. Here on the West Coast, his call was scheduled for 6:00 a.m., when many of the ID team members would have been awake for at least an hour in the DC area, even on a Sunday.

At the moment, he was in his townhouse's small but luxurious kitchen, sitting in his underwear at the round wooden table in its center, sipping on coffee he'd brewed.

It reminded him of Kelly's offer to make some for him last night.

Everything was likely to remind him of Kelly that day, but he had to make sure he remained professional in his thoughts and comments about her.

Comments shouldn't be a problem, at least not too much. Thoughts? After their amazing sex last night, as well as the night before, that was a whole different issue.

Both Alan's immediate superior officer, Director Walt Jones, and Judge Treena were to be in on this call. Alan knew what it would be about—a status report on how he was doing in obtaining usable evidence against City Councilman Stan Grodon, and another kind of report about Kelly Ladd, what she was doing and how successful Alan was in getting her to start complying with the promises she had made and return to the identity they had created for her.

Alan was not used to taking on an assignment and being unsuccessful, but at the moment he was batting close to zero.

Oh, sure, he'd developed an adequate working relationship with Stan. The guy seemed to trust him as a security provider. They'd had conversations, though mostly about meetings and who'd be there and how strong the security should be.

Nothing on a more friendly level, which wasn't a surprise. And so far there'd been little Alan had seen, few people he had run into, that might help him in his quest for eyewitness testimony against Stan, or better yet, hard evidence of his murdering, and disposing of, his long-missing wife.

And telling his superiors about his working with Kelly to seek out that evidence wasn't the best idea. He would have to be careful about his comments, too.

He took another sip of coffee, sighed and stood. He could at least start getting ready for the day. He wouldn't be on official duty at Government Plaza, but was scheduled for a couple of walk-throughs to ensure all looked in order. Dodd would be doing the same, so he'd be able to compare notes with his fellow security guy.

But unsurprisingly, no city council meetings were scheduled, so the likelihood of his accomplishing anything of importance to his real assignment was limited.

He went into the bathroom and shaved the dark shadow off his face. If he'd had no security duty at all that day, he'd have left it, since it was comfortable and many women liked that look these days.

He wondered what Kelly would think of him wearing a hint of a beard…

By the time he was finished, he was expecting the call to come at any minute, so he strolled back into the kitchen, poured hot coffee into his empty cup, added milk and only waited for a few seconds before his phone rang.

"Hello?" he said.

"Alan, this is Judge Treena," said a familiar female voice, strong and incisive.

"I'm here, too," said Director Walt Jones.

For a minute or so, they traded small talk about the weather. Since it was fall, it was warm on the West

Coast and cooler in DC, and a lot drier here than at the ID Division headquarters.

Then they started getting into the reasons for the call. They went over all that Alan had done. He kept it upbeat and positive. "I'm working on other angles to learn more from some of Grodon's assistants and co-workers," he assured them.

"And Kelly Ladd?" Judge Treena said in a barbed tone that raked over Alan's conscience. "What's she doing?"

"I'm still finding her useful." Alan looked at the ceiling as he spoke. Useful? Yeah, she was that and a whole lot more. "And no one recognizes her, so the Transformation Unit has done a great job."

He didn't want to lay it on too thick, but a little compliment wouldn't hurt.

"Mmm-hmm," the judge grunted. "So you're failing to follow orders, too, and get her back here?"

"My first job is to collect evidence." Alan allowed his own tone to go brusque. "I'm to use all tools I can, and for now Kelly Ladd is among them. If she ever stops, I'll make it a priority to get her back to the location of her new identity."

"Then we don't need to send another operative there now to get that moving?" That was Director Jones.

"No, sir." Alan sucked in his breath. "Everything is under control."

It had to be. He would make sure of it.

He also had to do more. Step things up.

He hoped Kelly would learn something useful today in her meeting with Dora Shallner. And maybe, just maybe, he would run into someone new whom he could discreetly interrogate at Government Plaza.

* * *

First thing after waking up that morning, Kelly sat at her small kitchen table and booted up her laptop, as she often did.

These days it wasn't simply to check her email. No, she got into her assumed persona and looked at Eli's Facebook page, where she had seen the allusions to pain that had scared her—and brought her here.

Recently, at least since her arrival, Eli's posts tended to be typical teenage stuff, about school and friends and sports—sometimes in a teasing or silly tone, but nothing like the suffering she had detected before, not even around the time she had seen him at Government Plaza with a bruise on his face.

If his posts had always been like that, she wouldn't be here, and wouldn't have known about that bruise. But she wasn't about to leave again until she was certain he was okay. And, to whatever extent possible now that she had returned, she would help Alan find whatever they could to connect her horrible brother-in-law to poor, missing Andi's disappearance.

That would undoubtedly help Eli, too.

She logged in to Facebook under her cutesy ID that suggested she was a teenager like her nephew, and immediately checked his site.

Oh, no. There were no typical teenage topics or references as there had been recently.

Instead, Eli had just posted a little frowny face and said, "Weekends can suck. Where's Monday?" No explanation, not even to his friends who'd responded with questions. He had simply pressed Like to their comments.

What was going on?

Would Kelly learn anything today with an attempt as remote as getting together with a woman Stan seemed to have an interest in?

Kelly had an urge to call Alan to ask his advice. No, more to cry on his shoulder.

She did neither.

But she did get ready for her meeting with Dora later, not only dressing for it, but also priming her psyche to do all she could to learn something helpful.

On her drive up to the Blue View, Kelly tried to keep her breathing slow and even despite the eagerness and anxiety she felt.

Okay, she told herself. She had to be friendly and act really, really interested in the possibility of getting a job as a server at that upscale restaurant.

This time of day there wasn't much traffic heading up the mountainside toward the restaurant and adjoining shopping area, so despite that anxiety Kelly had no excuse for not getting there fairly quickly.

"I can do this," she said aloud as she parked her old clunker car in the nearly empty parking lot. "I *will* learn something to help Eli."

When she exited her vehicle and pressed the lock button on her key fob, she stood for a moment gazing at the chalet structure, now silhouetted against an azure sky instead of the growing twilight of last night. She looked down at her plain blue dress that she thought exemplified the person she wanted to portray that day: a wannabe server in a high-class restaurant instead of an ordinary town café. She wasn't too shabbily clad, but she wasn't overdressed, either.

Taking another deep breath, she strode toward the restaurant's front door.

A few people were inside, though fewer than were likely to be at the Haven at brunch time. She headed toward the tall wooden greeting stand, which had no one behind it.

She stood there for less than a minute before Dora approached from what Kelly assumed to be the kitchen. The shorter woman was also clad in a blue dress, but hers was a brighter shade and of a silky, dressier—and undoubtedly more expensive—material. As before, she walked with the grace of a model, and the smile on her face as she greeted Kelly appeared perfect and welcoming.

Now, if she only could get the woman talking about what she wanted to hear.

"Kelly, how wonderful to see you. Please come in and sit down. We'll have some coffee first, then I'll show you around and we can talk business."

"Hi, Dora." Kelly smiled back broadly. "Thank you so much. This is such a wonderful place. I really hope we can work things out for sometime in the future, at least."

Dora led her to a small table toward the back of the place and away from the view through the huge windows—away from prime real estate for customers. Her hostess gestured toward a female server who wasn't dressed quite as formally as the one who'd served them last night. She wore a yellow dress with matching low shoes, and the other servers Kelly saw around the dining area were similarly dressed.

Soon they had coffee in front of them, and Dora insisted on giving Kelly a croissant like her own—blueberry and delicious. Kelly wondered what the menu price would be.

Then they started talking.

Can I ask about Stan yet? Kelly's mind raced, but she told herself to be patient as she described her experience as a server, including at a restaurant in the area of her new identity, but not the actual place. Although Kelly realized that Judge Treena must know where she was—despite her still failing to call the wonderful woman who had helped her so much and explain what she had done and why—she didn't want word to get back to the judge in such a sideways manner.

They also discussed why Kelly had decided to move here, and how she had found her job at the Haven. Those she had answers for, since she had explained her move to Ella when she first applied for the job as just being in the mood for a change and always hearing wonderful things about California. And it was easy enough to describe why she had wanted a job in the downtown area of adorable Blue Haven.

When they were done with their croissants and coffee, Dora rose and motioned for Kelly to join her. "Let me give you a tour," she said.

Kelly was fine with the idea but hadn't yet ventured into Dora's relationship with, and interest in, Stan Grodon. It had been too much like an interview so far, which wasn't surprising. But Kelly would lead her into the topics she wanted to discuss…somehow.

Dora showed Kelly the Blue View's kitchen. It was vast and had so much more equipment than the Haven—all high-end, of course.

And all the while Kelly pondered how to aim the conversation in the direction she wanted. She wouldn't mention having seen Dora on a date with Stan at Tony's Lounge—at least, not unless it seemed warranted.

Dora showed her the multiple ovens and explained how they were used.

"Amazing," Kelly said. "We have a couple of large ovens at the Haven, but they're both pretty much used for the same kinds of things. At least I think so. I mostly just go into the kitchen to place and pick up orders." She paused to smile at Dora. "Speaking of the Haven again, I've seen you there with some members of city council, right? They seem very active in this town—or at least very hungry."

Dora motioned for Kelly to follow her, and they headed toward the nearest door out of the kitchen. "Yes, I know they eat at the Haven a lot and even order take-out for meals at their headquarters. Your restaurant is certainly convenient for them. But one reason I'm getting to know at least some members better is to encourage them to visit Blue View, maybe even throw an event here sometime soon."

"I get it." Kelly's mind swirled as Dora opened a door, and they entered a room with lockers along the walls and chairs in the middle.

"This is the break room. Servers can change clothes in the nearby restroom, and everyone's assigned a locker in here."

"That's so great," Kelly said. "We don't have anything like it at the Haven." How could she aim this discussion toward Stan, and whether Dora was really dating him? And, more important, had she met Eli, and if so, how had he seemed and what was Stan's attitude?

Maybe she could use her assumed relationship with Alan to get there.

"People are really friendly here in Blue Haven, aren't they?" Kelly made herself gush as they stood in the empty room. "I mean, well, there's a guy who works for the security company that takes care of Government Plaza who's been at the Haven and also at the plaza when I've taken food there. He's been really nice to me." *Like, he and I are screwing around*. But that was too blunt for her to say, of course.

"Oh, really? Well, yes, people do tend to be nice to one another here."

"I know I'm being nosy." Kelly looked slightly sideways toward the other woman while continuing to smile. "But you're so pretty and you've got so many things going for you. Does that include a boyfriend?"

Would Dora think she was getting too personal? After all, they weren't friends, and all this woman, whose family owned this elite restaurant, knew about Kelly was that she wanted a job here—and if she got it, Dora would become her boss.

"Well…kind of. I'd rather not say who, but I've been seeing one of those council members you've been serving food to." The smile on Dora's pretty face grew huge, and she looked down as if being coy, before aiming another glance up toward Kelly.

"Oh, I think I know who." Kelly's turn to act a little coy. "I've seen you two together and kind of wondered." She leaned slightly down toward Dora, even though they were alone, and said in a near-whisper, "It's that nice, smart councilman Stan Grodon, isn't it?"

Dora raised her light, perfectly arched brows a little. "I was hoping it wasn't obvious."

"I wouldn't say it was," Kelly responded. This conversation was moving just the way she wanted it to, and she had to keep herself from appearing too excited. "It's just I saw him sitting beside you and—"

She broke off. One of the female servers entered the room and said, "Hi, Dora. Just taking my break now. I've got to call my son's school. His teacher just left me a message, even though it's Sunday. Okay?"

"Sure," Dora said.

Having this conversation interrupted—and probably ended—so suddenly made Kelly feel as if she had been socked in the stomach.

Kelly calmed herself, though, as Dora and the server chatted for the next minute about why the teacher might have called, especially on a weekend.

She would get her conversation with Dora back on topic.

She had to.

Chapter 15

It was around eleven o'clock. Alan had been patrolling Government Plaza for half an hour this Sunday morning and would do one more round in the nearly empty building before leaving.

At the moment he was in the wide hallway on the ground floor, walking on its shining surface in his dressy yet comfortable rubber-soled shoes that went well with his security suit and tie.

He decided to stop in the small office used by the security team. He'd already seen Dodd wandering around upstairs when he was there, so if he ran into any of the others here they wouldn't include his closest buddy on the job. Their boss, Nevil, had been upstairs, too, but he'd said he was leaving.

Alan used the key card and opened the door. The room was empty except for the long tables containing the computers they used here.

He didn't want to take the time to get on one now. No, he would head back to his apartment in a while and could use his secure government-issued laptop to do any research he wanted.

He headed back out, closing the door behind him— and thinking, again, of Kelly. Not that she was off his mind much anyway, but right now she would be up at the Blue View talking to its part-owner Dora, trying to extract anything even the tiniest bit useful from her.

Was she succeeding?

If so, they would celebrate together.

If not, well, he would do all he could to comfort her—and set them both in another direction to start improving their results. He just had to figure out what that direction would be.

Or maybe he would follow his own orders and conscience and make her leave at last. Though that idea didn't please him now as much as it had when they had first met.

He saw another couple of security guys—Jorge and Prentice—walking down the hall toward him, and he waited to say hello.

"See anything out of order?" he asked them.

Both were around Alan's height, though Prentice was much stouter. They shook their heads and Jorge shrugged. "Nice gig today. Not much to do like on weekdays."

"Well, enjoy what's left of your time here." Alan had decided to vacate this floor and return to the area where the council offices were. At least it was more interesting, even if no one was there.

Only he was surprised, after heading up the steps, to see Councilman Stan Grodon walking toward him and away from his office, down the wide hall where council members and their assistants frequently roved on weekdays. But not weekends.

Today he wore a pale green shirt with the sleeves rolled up over black denim pants—not his usual formal councilman garb. His thinning hair was even a bit mussed over his round face, and he appeared to have chosen to look like an ordinary citizen rather than a mighty government guru.

"Hello, sir," Alan said, playing his role to the hilt. He was alone with his target. Could he use this meeting to get something useful?

He'd certainly be pleased to be able to tell Kelly that he had, even if she was successful, too.

"Hello. Everything secure around here?" Grodon probably didn't know, or remember, Alan's name, which was fine. But he did know Alan's role.

"That's what I'm checking. So far all looks good."

"Excellent. Keep up the good work. Oh, and you might let Hancock know we're starting to plan another event, probably off these premises—a luncheon maybe, or something else to hobnob with some of the local citizens."

In other words, a fund-raiser, at least for Grodon. Alan wouldn't ask questions now but would definitely be sure to be on duty that day to ensure security for the group—and keep an eye on Stan.

"Thanks for the warning, sir. I'll let my boss know." Hancock and his closest staff were fairly much a supervisory, hands-off group who relied on grunts like Alan was supposed to be, which was fine with him. But they would want to know so they'd be able to get a group—including Alan—together for the event.

Too bad Alan wouldn't be able to invite Kelly as a date to whatever it was, although depending on how it worked out, she might wind up as a server.

For now, he just nodded a farewell to the city councilman whose mind he wished he could read and continued down the hall. At the end he turned. Grodon had left.

And Alan decided not to follow him.

Hallelujah! Kelly thought. Dora had invited her into the restaurant's small office. Was she going to offer her a job?

If so, she would have to handle it carefully, request an amount of time to consider it—and also to consider how to gracefully refuse it.

She wanted to stay downtown, where all the action was.

And where she was more likely to get opportunities to see Eli. But maybe she could learn more about the situation between Dora and Stan now.

"Here we are." Dora pushed open a door with windows that were covered inside by curtains so the office beyond wasn't visible. She motioned for Kelly to precede her, which she did.

Inside, she saw a relatively small room filled with antique furniture, from wooden, carved file cabinets in the corner to a matching ornate desk in the center.

"Please have a seat." Dora gestured toward one of the two similarly antique chairs facing the desk. The chair she sat in behind it wasn't antique, but a modern desk chair.

"Thanks." Kelly complied, sitting at the edge of the chair she chose as if she were waiting eagerly for what was to come. "This is really nice." She looked around with a smile.

"Thank you."

Kelly didn't wait for Dora to begin their conversation. She decided to continue from where they'd been when they were interrupted in the break room. "This whole place is so amazing. Has…have you brought Councilman Grodon here for a meal?" She shot Dora a cutesy little smile, as if she wanted to continue pushing their budding friendship.

"Of course." Dora's expression fortunately just looked amused. "With some of his fellow council members, too."

"That's great. And what about his son? I met the boy at the council offices the other day when I brought in some food." This could be a mistake, if it got back to Stan that some mere server was getting so personal with Eli.

But it was exactly what Kelly needed. What she was after.

"No, he hasn't been here." Dora's tone wasn't quite as chummy as before. "Stan introduced me to him once when the kid was at the plaza and on his way out with a friend and his mother." Then Stan was aware of Eli's internship at the plaza, even though Eli apparently attempted to avoid his father.

Did Eli seem okay then? Kelly longed to ask. *What was Stan's attitude?*

More questions she didn't dare ask flooded Kelly's mind, and Dora seemed to sense something, judging by her curious and somewhat chilly glance.

"Anyway, the kid seemed nice enough. Maybe a little awed by his dad and his power in Blue Haven. I kind of got the sense he wanted to stay quiet and figure out what his dad wanted. Impress him, maybe. Be a perfect little angel, even at that age. Maybe I'll see him again sometime." Did she want to? Would she be interested in acquiring a stepson?

If so, how would she act with Eli?

And if Kelly had her druthers, it wouldn't happen, since Stan wouldn't be able to marry Dora. Not while he was in prison.

Dora leaned over the desk toward Kelly. "Now let's get down to business."

Kelly's heart dropped. She'd learned probably all she was going to about Eli from Dora. He'd apparently given the impression of complete subservience, but little else.

Although that did tell her something about his relationship with his domineering, cruel—and murderous—father.

Oh, Eli, I'll figure something out, her mind cried, even as she listened to Dora.

"Now, here's the thing," the restaurant owner was saying. "I like you, Kelly. I think you'd fit in well here."

Uh-oh. Kelly's mind spun as she tried to figure out how to nicely say no.

"But like I mentioned before, the problem is that we're already overstaffed at this moment."

Great! Then she didn't need to make up excuses, at least not now.

"Oh," she said, trying to sound despondent.

"I'll certainly keep you in mind the next time we have an opening, though. They seem to come up unexpectedly, as you probably know."

"Yes. Sure. I'll just hope one comes up when I can

accept a position with you. Thanks for thinking of me." Kelly tried to sound as if she could hardly wait for the job sometime in the future…maybe. "Anyway, I'd better go now. But I'll look forward to talking with you again."

She rose then, trying not to look relieved, and allowed Dora to show her back into the restaurant and toward the door.

Alan was getting ready to leave. His job for the day here was pretty much over, so he headed down to the ground floor once more.

There, he popped into the security office to sign out. Dodd was sitting at a computer, and the two of them exchanged quick barbs—and notes about what they had and hadn't seen that day.

"You ready to leave?" Dodd asked. "I am, almost. Good day, though. I asked to be here. Sundays are pretty dead around here. Piece of cake to patrol then."

"It sure is." Even though Alan was curious why he'd seen Grodon here. But the councilman could be a dedicated member of city government on top of all the questionable activities he engaged in, so maybe he'd actually done something productive here today.

Not that Alan believed that.

"See you tomorrow?" Dodd asked as Alan waved and started to leave.

"Yep, see you then."

He walked into the hallway and toward the rear exit, to the parking lot where he had left his car.

And he was *very* interested to see Stan Grodon at the far end of the lot near a car that did not look as ritzy as he expected the councilman to own.

But a guy got out of the driver's seat then and stood up, talking to Grodon.

It was Grodon's assistant, Paul Tirths, whom Alan had met but who had left town shortly thereafter.

Alan immediately thought of something he could ask the councilman so he could draw closer to the two men—but Tirths got back into the driver's seat, and Grodon went to the passenger's side and got in.

Well, Tirths was back. He was the person who'd initially been on Shereen Alsop's side when her sister disappeared, then did an about-face without providing any ability to call him as an eyewitness or obtain any other kind of proof from him.

But this was definitely something to talk to Kelly about.

And to dig in further to see what useful info Tirths could provide…possibly with a little persuasion.

On her way back toward town, Kelly carefully navigated the narrow road with one side providing a majestic view of the water. She thought about calling Alan but decided against it. She knew he was on some kind of limited security patrol around the plaza today and didn't want to interrupt him.

She had hoped to have something useful to report to him, though, about Dora's knowledge of Eli. But what she'd learned hadn't been especially helpful, only that Stan introduced his son to people he met, at least sometimes. Maybe if Dora and Stan were more of an item she'd have gotten to know Eli better, but the restaurateur's attitude toward her potential romantic interest's child didn't seem especially positive.

Kelly's contact with Dora was turning out to be a

dead end, although she would continue to cultivate it in case something more came of it later—perhaps if Stan and Dora were actually more of an item than she believed.

The narrow mountain roadway was ending, and Kelly would soon be on a more substantial road. Where should she go now?

She wasn't scheduled to work. She certainly wasn't getting together with Alan.

And she unfortunately had no legitimate reason to drive past Stan's—and Eli's, and formerly Andi's—home, although she might do that anyway and just claim to be sightseeing in her new town if anyone noticed.

For now, though? An idea came to her, not that it was likely to be particularly useful. But it wouldn't hurt to remind herself what that piece of property looked like that Stan had been trying to help real estate broker Jerome Baranka sell to the National Ecological Research Administration, and see if it appeared any different from the last time she had seen it. After all, it was near the water and not far from here.

Well, maybe it would hurt. It would remind her a lot of Andi, and her sister's fight with her husband...

But it was a reminder that she could live with, since her sister's disappearance and likely death had been the result.

At the intersection at the base of the hill, she turned right on Coast Road, in the direction of that property.

The road here curved some since it followed the shoreline, but was much straighter and wider than the one up to the Blue View. It was a commercial area, with restaurants and beach clubs, grocery stores and places that sold beach clothing.

The site that Andi had represented was a short distance away, and Kelly reached it fairly quickly. It was on the water side of the road and remained empty. Apparently not even Andi's employers had found an appropriate buyer for it after NERA had passed on it.

Kelly drove by more stores, offices and small businesses—and stopped at the traffic light at the corner of the site that had been the subject of such contention way back when.

A long, two-story office building was located there. It appeared under construction and not yet occupied. Some of the internal structure still showed, and wood was nailed over what would be the windows.

But a sign posted in the front said it was the future site of the National Ecological Research Administration.

Kelly drew in her lips and glared, as if the building were alive and responsible, somehow, for what had happened to Andi.

There was a parking lot on the near side of the building that contained a few cars. She drove past slowly. Fortunately, although there was traffic on the other side of the road, there was no one behind her.

As she drove by, she noticed three people exit from the building's front door, all men.

And Kelly gasped as she recognized each of them: Stan Grodon, Jerome Baranka and Paul Tirths.

Paul. Initially her friend and helper in learning what Stan had done with his wife… Kelly's sister.

And then nearly as much of an enemy as Stan.

He'd been away when she first arrived here. Now he was back.

Was he more likely to recognize her than her own brother-in-law? They had spent a lot of time together collaborating and commiserating about Stan, who he was and how murderous he had become.

Until Paul had become his boss's biggest advocate once more. His being here with Stan and Baranka indicated where his loyalties still lay…for now.

He might have the information Kelly wanted, the information Alan was after that would provide evidence against Stan, and perhaps lead to Andi.

But how could newcomer to Blue Haven, restaurant server Kelly Ladd, extract any of that from Paul?

She had to let Alan know. And then she would work with him to get the results they both sought.

Chapter 16

Alan was in his car still in the plaza parking lot checking his email when his phone signaled he had received a text message.

It was from Kelly. Would like to talk to you, it said.

Why did he have a sense there was a lot of emotion behind those benign words? Maybe because he had seen Stan and Paul Tirths and intended to let Kelly know. Maybe he anticipated some kind of emotional communication with her.

Or was he just considering how best to let her know? If so, he'd tamp down any emotion. He was on the job. His real job. Staying fully calm was the only way to go.

Now's good for me, he texted back. You?

He wasn't surprised when his phone rang almost immediately.

"Hi, Alan? Is this an okay time to talk?" Kelly's voice sounded breathless, as if she were running.

"Sure. You all right? Where are you?"

"In my car. How about you?"

"Just leaving the plaza."

"How about if I come and pick you up? I need to talk to you."

He could hardly refuse, not that he wanted to. All the emotion he'd been anticipating, and even more, seemed to emanate from her at this distance, wherever she was. He needed to know why. And if he could help her, soothe her, then all the better.

"Sure. I'll wait on the corner for you."

"I'll be about ten minutes," she said.

"That's fine. Take your time." He didn't want her speeding, especially if she was upset. Better that she arrive here safely so they could talk than for her to get stopped by cops...or worse.

"See you in a few."

Kelly took Alan's words about taking her time to heart. Even though she was no longer on mountain roads and the streets here were relatively empty, she'd been unexpectedly walloped by the sight of those three men, one in particular.

She had to figure out, with Alan, what to do next.

Before she picked him up, she needed to calm herself, determine how best to tell Alan what—who—she had seen and consider suggestions for their next steps.

Alan. Alan, Alan. Damn it, but the man was now permeating her brain, in her thoughts, much too much.

Yet there wasn't a lot she could do on her own right now, in this alternate persona, to get Paul Tirths to open up about what he knew. Or to get Stan talking, admitting what he had done.

No, someone trained in covert security operations like Alan was a much better bet. She had to remain a poor, scared restaurant server to protect herself by deception.

But she, and not Alan, had to come up with a way to protect and save her nephew.

She'd been driving slowly. It was early afternoon now, but she was finally downtown.

In another five minutes she reached the plaza. She saw Alan nearly immediately, standing on the corner of Main Street and Pacific Avenue looking down at his phone. He appeared so businesslike standing there, even wearing a suit and tie despite the fact it was the weekend and the council was probably not meeting.

He looked like one handsome, sexy businessman, standing out in the small group of pedestrians walking by on the sidewalk. If she hadn't known who he was, she might have figured he was conducting some kind of lucrative transaction on his phone, even on a Sunday.

More likely, he was either communicating with someone else at the CIU or checking for some piece of information that would help him achieve his under-cover goal here.

Either way, she felt glad. He was, indirectly, here for her. He would help her figure it all out.

At least she hoped he would.

Slowly, since there was more traffic here than closer to the shore, she inched her way to the curb near him, then turned on her signal to show she was stopping. Fortunately, although there was a yellow line at the curb, other vehicles could get around her. She lowered the passenger window, ready to call out to Alan, but she didn't have to. He strode quickly in her direction and opened the door.

"Hi," he said, getting in.

"Hi." She knew she must sound relieved, even though she'd told herself to keep her cool, act like his completely professional colleague. "Thanks for meeting me."

"You knew I would." Which was true. They had formed a bond, after all—one that was more than just professional. "What's going on?"

She couldn't continue to sit here at the curb. But driving while they held this discussion of something that definitely spun her insides probably wasn't a great idea.

"Let's go to my place, okay? I'll make us some coffee, and we'll talk."

Of course Alan would have agreed to go someplace private, like Kelly's apartment or even his own. But either would have taken a while, and just looking at her, watching her chest rise and fall at a much faster rate than normal—and he certainly enjoyed watching that part of her, even clothed—it was obvious that the sooner they talked, the better.

"That would be fine," he said, "but I'd rather we talk now. Here, pull into one of the metered spots on the street and I'll pay for parking. We'll take a short walk together and talk. And if anyone we know sees us, all the better for our cover story. Okay?"

Her glance toward him appeared both amused and troubled, but she nodded and parked at one of the nearest spaces.

He would have gone over to open her door, but she

beat him to it. He used a credit card to feed the meter. He doubted they'd be there long, but he added enough to give them an hour, just in case.

There was a surprising number of pedestrians around them, walking around this area that was all government buildings. Maybe some were tourists, which the Blue Haven government encouraged, and these buildings certainly had attractive exteriors. Most were of the same faux marble look as the main plaza building, with pointed roofs and rows of decorative windows beneath them.

But few pedestrians seemed to stop and gawk at the structures. They walked by, perhaps moving to and from the nearest shopping areas only a couple of blocks away.

That was also where the Haven was located. He started walking in that direction, and Kelly joined him without question or protest.

"So tell me," he said.

Despite Kelly's rational thinking and her intention to remain unemotional as she talked about whom she'd seen, and in the blatant company of the man he had at one time accused of murdering her sister, it got to her. She walked beside Alan, staring at the mostly smooth sidewalk, trying to remain calm as she told him where she had been and why. "I only wanted to take a look at those properties again since I was in the area," she said, knowing her voice was low and unsteady. "I didn't imagine I'd see anyone I knew there, although perhaps seeing the real estate guy Baranka was no surprise. But Stan. And Paul."

Her voice rose on the final two names, and she bit

her lip—only to feel Alan's arm go around her shoulders. She turned to look up into his sympathetic gaze.

"I saw Stan and Paul, too, a while ago at the plaza. They were getting into a car, and I had no opportunity to talk to them. But I'll find a way. I promise."

"And can you promise you'll get Paul to spill all he knows about Andi?" Kelly didn't mean for her words to come out so emotional and almost accusatory. She trusted Alan—or at least trusted that he would do everything in his power to get the answers, and evidence, they sought.

"I do promise, Kelly." That surprised her.

"But how can you? I mean—"

"It's my job. Remember?" His smile looked wry, and she had an urge to reach up and touch his taut lips. Better yet, kiss them—as inappropriate as that was.

"Of course I remember. But—"

"And now it's more than my job. I want—no, need—to do it to help my girlfriend, don't I? You."

Kelly felt her eyes widen. "But it's all for show. I'm not—"

Alan stopped, causing her to stop walking, too. "Some is for show, sure. But I like you. I care about you. And if doing what I was sent here to do helps you, then all the better. We'll get what we're after, though it might take a while longer. You'll see."

Kelly inhaled deeply. She wanted to believe him. To trust him. But he wasn't the only person involved in this.

She didn't trust those he needed to go after. And so far, he'd had no success since his arrival here.

But now there were two of them working on it together. Surely that would make a difference.

"Thank you," she said, choosing to fully buy into what he was saying.

"You're welcome." He bent down, and their lips met in a short but heated kiss. When he pulled back, he said, "We can talk about this more. I want to hear your thoughts. Let's grab dinner, then go to your place."

The idea of that nearly made Kelly smile despite her mixed feelings. But she didn't respond immediately, mulling the idea over for a moment. The idea of getting together with him for another evening—another night—sounded wonderful. It also sounded wrong.

She didn't want him to see the horribly confused and upset fool she suddenly was inside. Or maybe he had seen it—she hadn't really been hiding it well—and that was the reason for his suggestion.

"Let's do dinner," she finally agreed. "I think I need to be alone later tonight, though."

She wondered if he would try to convince her otherwise.

Alan suggested Juan's, a popular Mexican restaurant that wasn't far from the Haven. Kelly seemed fine with it, and she drove them there.

One good thing about the place was that its walls and outer windows were lined with booths with high backs, so there was a feeling of at least a little privacy when they were seated.

"Margarita?" Alan immediately asked Kelly, sitting on the wooden bench across from her. He intended to have one.

"Strawberry," she said with a nod.

As at the Haven, the women servers all wore the same outfits, but here it was loose knee-length skirts in different colors, and white blouses with colorful embroidery around the neckline. After their margaritas were served, Kelly ordered a taco salad and Alan asked for a beef burrito.

Then they were alone together.

"I'd been planning on calling you later anyway," he said, "and not just so we could make a date and be seen together."

"Really? I thought that was the whole purpose of our getting together." Her smile looked sad, perhaps as though she actually believed that—despite what they had done in no one else's presence.

He had an urge to slip off his bench, move onto hers and hold her closely to him.

But the timing didn't feel right.

"Only part of it," he said without moving. But before he could give her the small bit of information he had, their server came over with some tortilla chips and salsa, placing them on the table.

"Enjoy," she said.

"Thanks," Kelly said with a big smile. Of course she would be more than polite to a server at another restaurant.

She took a chip and dipped it into the salsa, then took a bite. "Good. Spicy but not overly so."

Keeping things impersonal and far from their common goal might be fine most of the time, but under the circumstances Alan believed that they really needed to talk, to trade information.

He nevertheless grabbed a couple of chips and dipped them, too.

Then he said, "When I saw Paul Tirths and Stan today, my first instinct was to follow them, but even though I was leaving the plaza I was still too far from my car. Now I know where they were heading. But I want to learn why." He watched the expression on Kelly's lovely face as he spoke.

She looked as if she wanted to say something, although she didn't at first. She reached for her margarita and took a sip. "Me, too," she finally said. And then, her eyes wide and sorrowful, she asked, "How are we going to do this, Alan? *Are* we going to do this?" She glanced around as if sure people were listening in.

"We are," he assured her. "But this isn't the time or place to figure it out. However—" He paused, and she regarded him expectantly. "Stan told me about a big afternoon party the council is planning for its members and apparently some townsfolk, too. I suspect both our targets will be there, and they'll be needing some security. Now that Paul is back, I'm going to get to know him, put into effect the plan I'd been devising when he disappeared. We're going to become great friends."

"Really?" Her smile this time was bright but skeptical.

"Oh, he'll think so. Even if he doesn't, I'll get him to reveal all by talking to me about Andi—and also the attempts on Shereen's life. I can probably get him immunity but only if he helps."

"That is so great!"

Alan couldn't help feeling proud that he'd caused Kelly to smile. She believed in him. Or at least she wanted to.

Now all he had to do was deliver.

Could he?

Judge Treena would undoubtedly help with the immunity angle, at least.

As Alan took a healthy swig of his margarita, their server returned with their meals. For the rest of their dinner, they talked mostly about their lives there, nothing relating to what they were really up to. Kelly seemed to relax, even tease him a bit with her sexy expressions at times, and allusions to their seeing each other in different ways, too.

When they were finished, Kelly tried to pay the bill. "It's my turn," she said.

"But I'm on an expense account for anything relating to my assignment, so it's always my turn." Plus, he knew he earned more than she did. And he hadn't footed the expense of moving here.

They soon left the restaurant. Alan regretted that they weren't spending more time together that night, but he wouldn't push Kelly.

After they were in her car so she could drive him back to the plaza to get his own vehicle, she turned to look at him.

"It might be a dumb idea, but I thought earlier, before I saw Stan and the others, that I'd drive by Stan's house, just pretend I was sightseeing around the area if anyone spotted me. I'd like to do it now, with you along, if that's okay."

"Sure it is," he said. "And it's not a dumb idea. I've been by there, but you can give me more information about the location that I may be able to use. Let's go."

Chapter 17

The drive to, and through, the lovely residential neighborhood about two miles from downtown was familiar to Kelly.

Boy, was it.

She had lived nearby, too, in an area closer to the school where she—Shereen—had been a fourth-grade teacher. But she had visited Andi, her husband and her son often at their much more affluent home.

She had wanted, intended, to come by here from the moment she set foot back in town, but she had been afraid to.

She wasn't afraid of Stan or of being seen here, but of what her emotions would do.

That was a major reason she had invited Alan to join her. He was an outsider to the situation as well as someone on her side, someone she could rely on.

A rock, when she was having a hard time controlling her emotions.

"So you lived in this neighborhood, too?" Alan peered out the windshield toward the nearest of the large homes. It had white stucco walls and multiple archways beneath its peaked roof, as did others along this street, although their exterior colors varied.

Andi's, Stan's and Eli's—no, just Stan's and Eli's now—was an attractive beige, just one block away now, on Guilder Street.

"On its fringes," she told Alan. "My salary as a teacher certainly beat what I'm getting now, but it didn't compare with a city councilman and real estate agent combined." She paused, then added, "Not to mention the additional income I'm fairly sure Stan receives from bribes and other under-the-table deals."

She hadn't visited the area of her former apartment, not even to drive by and check it out. She'd been nearly run over there—more than once.

She had no interest in seeing it again.

The roads here were fairly straight, wide enough for two-way traffic and for people to park at the curbs. The sidewalks were lined with trees, mostly pines.

Oh, yes, this area was delightful. Or at least that was the way she had once regarded it.

She reached the block where Stan and Eli still lived. She had checked a public records website, and fortunately the information was there. The trees still stood like tall sentries.

Kelly realized she was holding her breath. She was anticipating something that could never happen again.

She visualized Andi on the front porch, using her tablet to go over the latest real estate listings in the area.

Unless...no, if Andi were alive somewhere, she would have contacted Shereen long before now. She had always been a wonderful, thoughtful, kind big sister.

Kelly had been driving slowly but now reduced her speed even more. Many parking spaces on both sides of the street were filled, but at the moment they were the only car on the road. She saw gardeners at a couple of houses, but no one outside who appeared to be a resident.

Then there they were, right outside the Grodon home.

No one was on the porch, although the nice metal outdoor furniture she remembered was still there. No one was in the yard, either. Not Andi, and not even Eli.

Was her nephew inside? Maybe. It was, after all, a Sunday evening. If only she could reach out to him mentally, get him to dash out the front door and...

"Are you okay?" Alan's voice drew her abruptly back to reality.

"More or less," she said, hearing the catch in her tone. She sounded as if she was about to cry.

She felt like she was about to cry, too.

"Sounds like less to me. Keep on going, and I'll take over the driving once we're on another block out of sight of this place." He didn't ask her okay on that, but it sounded good to her. She could still concentrate on driving, but tears had started flowing slowly down her face, so she wasn't sure how safe she'd be.

"Okay," she rasped.

She continued driving for another couple of blocks, going just a bit faster than before. She pulled down a side street. After parking, she went around to the passenger seat, and in a minute, Alan was the one driving. But when they left the residential neighborhood he turned in the opposite direction from downtown.

"We need to take you to your car," she said.

"Not now. In the morning. Right now, you're coming home with me."

She felt shocked—but at the same time, relieved. She wouldn't be alone.

And yet, the last two nights they had been together, the closeness they had engaged in…it was amazing and delightful…well, she didn't want to even think about that now. Or at least not much.

"I appreciate that," she began, "but—"

"Don't worry. I won't touch you. I just think some company is in order tonight. We can play video games or watch movies if you want. But you're staying with me."

Alan pulled Kelly's car into the driveway at the front of his triplex unit and parked. She exited and just stood there looking up at his place. She was wearing an attractive blue dress, and her curly brown hair framed her face that was as beautiful as always, despite its pallor this day.

"Very nice," she said. He tried to view his home from her perspective, both in her past life as Shereen, and now as Kelly.

"Thanks," he responded, realizing, after seeing where Shereen's family lived, that this area was nice but impersonal, where people who were employed with good jobs rented without necessarily intending to stay very long. Then there was Kelly's apartment in the part of town where people probably aspired to those kinds of jobs and relocation to a place like this.

He took her hand and led her to the front door, up a slight rise that held a drought-tolerant garden with pebbles as a base and a few cacti and similar plants. He unlocked the door and motioned for her to enter first.

He tried to see his entry hall from her perspective. It was somewhat elegant, with an antique mirror hung across from the door so he could watch himself—and anyone else—coming in. There were two doorways. One led into the moderate-sized living room on this floor. The other led to the hall from which the stairway to the top two stories rose, and also to the kitchen and a back door to the tiny, fenced backyard.

It worked for the person he had to be here in Blue Haven.

"Very nice," Kelly said as, holding her hand once more, he led her into the living room. There, he sat down beside her on the beige sectional couch that faced the one thing he had bought here for his own use: a large, wall-mounted television. There was a low coffee table in front of the couch and not much else in this room.

He'd originally planned to try to divert Kelly's attention from what she had seen, what she had remembered, on her sorrowful trip down memory lane in that other area of Blue Haven. Now, though, he looked into her sad brown eyes, which glimmered with unshed tears.

"Wait here and I'll get you some wine," he said.

"I'll come with you. I'd like to see your kitchen, too."

He wouldn't argue with that. He led her down the other hallway, then observed how she looked out the window into what passed as his tiny backyard while he poured their wine into round-bottomed glasses without stems. He handed one to her. "Let's go back to the living room, okay?"

"Sure."

She was being much too pliant for the Kelly he had come to know. That worried him. Made him feel sad, too—enough that he knew he had to do something.

Watching the news or even some kind of sitcom on TV wouldn't do it. Nor would a video game.

No, she needed some kind of catharsis, although it was undoubtedly premature since they'd had no results so far.

But even though complete mental relief might not be achievable, he might be able to help her take a step in the right direction.

Once she was settled on one end of the couch, her wineglass clutched in her right hand and her eyes staring down at it, Alan said, "Tell me about her, Kelly. No, both of them. Tell me some of the good things you remember about your sister and Eli. And then we can talk some more about how to move forward."

This was the last thing Kelly had anticipated.

Not that both of her dearest relatives weren't always on her mind. But talk about them? About all she was missing?

"I'm not sure that's a good idea," she said softly, then added, "but I'll try."

She started way back, how she and Andi had been raised by their parents in Long Beach. "She was always a really nice big sister, protective of me if anyone started hassling me—even our parents."

She said that both her mother and father had been

schoolteachers, which was what inspired her career, although both taught middle grades, not elementary.

"They both had tempers, but apparently saved any temper tantrums to level at us when they got home." Kelly smiled, despite the fact that it wasn't her fondest memory of them.

Andi had been six years older than her and had left town to get her degree in business while Kelly remained at home. That was where she had met Stan, who was also studying business. "He seemed an okay guy then." Kelly shook her head. "Unlike now."

Then she had to describe the first time her life fell apart. "Our parents were killed in a car crash not long after Andi married Stan. I used my inheritance to get a teaching degree, and when I graduated I just couldn't return to Long Beach, so I moved to Blue Haven to be with my sister, who welcomed me."

That was around the time Stan's interest in politics was born—and so was Eli.

Kelly had told these basics to Judge Treena's identity team, but the only part she had gone into detail about was how things had started deteriorating after that.

"I loved Eli from the moment he was born." Kelly choked on her words, or maybe it was the tears that had started falling down her cheeks. "I babysat him every moment I could, spent time in their house even though I'd rented my own apartment after landing my teaching job. Stan wasn't particularly discreet about how he treated Andi, essentially taking an entirely outdated position that, since he was the man, he was in charge. Andi loved him, though, and sometimes laughed at his nastiness and gave him big kisses even when I was there, to get him to back down." She paused, closing her eyes. "But her laughing it off stopped working after Stan won his first election to city council. Then he made it clear he really did consider himself the boss of the family. That was also when he apparently decided that he was above the law and could accept bribes or whatever he chose to do. That's when their real arguments started. Their face-off about the real estate deal and Andi's attempt to sell property to the same federal agency as one of Stan's donors…"

Kelly choked up and couldn't continue. Not then, even though Alan had moved so he now sat right beside her on the sofa, his arm around her. She lay her head on his shoulder, swallowing her sobs.

"Eli grew up in the middle of all this. He—he saw his parents fight, even more than our parents had. I took him out for dinner and to the park and everywhere I could to try to protect him. He was like my own child. Then—then his mother disappeared. And after that, I had to disappear on him, too, to stay alive."

She couldn't talk anymore, not then. Alan, who had remained silent but shot encouraging and sympathetic glances her way, now held her close as she cried her heart out.

"I'm very sorry, Shereen," he said, using her real name, which was appropriate but made her cry all the more. "I can't fix everything, but you can be sure I'll do everything to make sure that Stan pays for what he did, and that you get to help Eli from now on."

So many times during Kelly's story, Alan had an urge to kiss her into silence. It was painful even to listen to her, and he regretted making her talk about it.

Would recalling everything help or hurt her? He hoped the former, but that remained to be seen.

He'd asked it of her because he thought it would ultimately help her to put the worst behind her. Now he felt her pain, as if it exited her skin and entered his body, just because he was holding her.

He cared for her. Too much, and not just because they were working together.

That meant he had to back off, physically as well as emotionally. She was still a colleague of sorts, one who failed to comply with the rules she had promised to follow. He understood it, but now fought his instinct not to buy into it.

He didn't let her go, though. He buried his face in the softness of her hair, feeling its waves stroke his cheeks as she trembled while she cried. The scent was light and floral, and her nearness, the utter femininity of her body, made his own react—oh, so very inappropriately.

Maybe he should have just taken her to her apartment. That way he could have simply given her a final good-night hug and left.

Yeah, and feel even more like a heel.

"I'm sorry, Kelly," he murmured against her head. "I thought this would help you, but instead—"

"It did," she protested, pulling back a little until she was looking up into his eyes. Then she amended, "It will, at least. I've been trying not to think about it too much, but I always do. Now that you've been so kind to let me share it this way, I won't feel nearly as bad about it. I hope." She pulled back even farther, and those gorgeous brown eyes of hers suddenly appeared more fierce than sad. "We're going to get him. We're going to find Andi, learn what he did to her and put him away forever."

It wasn't a question but a statement, and it made him smile. Her return smile looked almost like a challenge, as if she dared him to contradict her.

Of course he didn't. He couldn't. That was his job here, too.

It was also his goal because he wanted to do it, for Kelly's sake. And because the miserable excuse for a man had also tried to kill her.

Without thinking, he bent his head to kiss that smile.

Kelly responded. Did she ever. Her kiss was as forceful as her expression had been. Her tongue reached out to engage his, as if they were dueling for who could exercise theirs most sensually.

He had an urge to touch her all over—using his tongue for some of it. But he had promised, when he said he would bring her here…

She was the one to start touching him as they remained on the couch. She rubbed his chest first, and then her hand traveled downward.

His erection was already thick and hard by then, and her grip outside his pants only enlarged it. He considered leading her upstairs, but why? His couch would be a perfectly good location for what he wanted to do to her. What he wanted them to do together.

He pulled away so he could stand up and draw her up in front of him. He hadn't studied her dress from the perspective of getting it off before. Now he did, even as she started unbuttoning his shirt.

They were colleagues, collaborators, in this as much as anything else. Soon, they both were naked.

He looked at her lovely body even as he continued

to stroke it. Fortunately, even though he had felt certain nothing like this would occur tonight, he had a condom in his wallet for emergencies—like this one. He bent to pull it out, and Kelly reached for it.

"Let me," she rasped.

In moments, he was sheathed. And even hotter and more eager than he had been the last two nights they had been together.

"Please, Alan," she breathed, and he soon was inside her—with the sole intention of pleasing her.

Chapter 18

Afterward, Kelly lay on the couch, Alan's delight-fully heavy weight on top of her.

She hadn't intended this tonight. Well, she hadn't started out intending to make love with him the other two nights, either, but this time she had wanted a re-spite.

Or so she'd believed.

"Am I squashing you?" he asked roughly into her ear.

"Probably, but it feels good."

She liked the sound of his laugh. The feel of him on her. His company, and his sympathy.

Even so...

"Alan, this was wonderful. But...well, I still want to spend the rest of the night alone, at my place."

She felt his whole body stiffen, and then he slid off

her onto the floor. "I thought you wanted this, too. I certainly didn't mean to—"

"I did want it. Or at least it felt really good, even though I hadn't intended it. But I let myself spout all those emotions, then somehow must have thought I could wash them all away by shutting up and having sex with you. But everything is still there, inside me. As much as I enjoyed this, I don't want to talk about it anymore. I think I'd better just go home."

As if she had a real home to go to. But she did have the apartment she rented here, where she could be alone.

And rehash everything she had talked about all over again...the idea felt horrible. But it was all there, no matter what she did. And if she stayed here, she might start talking once more—and she wouldn't allow herself to discuss it any further.

Plus, as wonderful as the sexual encounter with Alan had been, if she stayed, they might do it again. And she just couldn't right now, not if she wanted to remain sane. Or at least as sane as Kelly Ladd could possibly be.

"If that's what you really want," Alan said. She was about to insist when he continued. "But what I really want is to try to help you through this night, not by touching you again, or having more sex, but just by holding you. Being there for you. Could we give that a try? If it doesn't feel right to you, you can tell me anytime and I will take you back to your place, work out the car situation in the morning, whatever you want."

That sounded so heavenly. So perfect. She would have caring company with no strings attached. Someone who would be there for her this night in case her thoughts returned to the bad stuff and she began crying again.

"Okay," she said huskily. "Let's give it a try."

A short while later, they were in his bed together. Alan had given Kelly a long gray T-shirt to wear since he realized she wouldn't feel comfortable wearing nothing, especially when they had agreed to a hands-off policy for the rest of the night. Her dress—and her underwear—wouldn't have worked well, either.

He'd donned a comfortable pair of pj's that also let nothing show on his part. At the moment, he was far from being turned on anyway. He was too worried about her.

Now, she lay beside him in the dark beneath the blanket atop the plain beige sheets on his queen-size mattress. It was possibly as far away as she could get.

Her short, sometimes uneven breathing, told him that she remained as awake as he was.

"Kelly," he finally whispered.

"Yes?" Her response was immediate, almost as if she had been expecting him to say something.

"May I hold you? I don't mean in a sexual way. I'd just like the body contact. And if you feel uncomfortable, you can always pull away."

"Well, okay."

She turned toward him, and they both moved toward the center of the bed. He moved onto his side beneath the blanket and reached out, maneuvering so that he was nearly on his stomach against her, his arm around her.

Did he dare kiss her?

He figured that wouldn't hurt, so he lifted his head and moved till his lips found hers.

Their kiss wasn't exactly chaste, but it didn't evoke thoughts of further sensual pleasure. At least not *too* much sensual pleasure.

And Alan was pleased to feel the soft rise and fall of Kelly's chest, hear her breathing grow deeper and more steady, as she finally fell asleep a short while later.

Upon waking, Kelly had wished she didn't have to go to work that day, but there she was anyway, starting to wait on customers for breakfast in the Haven's crowded and noisy dining room.

Alan had gently awakened her early enough for them to get his car back without the likelihood of encountering too many witnesses. Though even if they were seen, it would fit with the story they were encouraging about their alleged relationship. But Kelly didn't want to have to deal with any suggestive or teasing comments from anyone she knew, so after Alan had showered and dressed for his job, she had dropped him off at the plaza.

Then she had returned to her apartment in the dress she had worn last night, showered and changed into her Haven uniform.

Right now, she was glad the restaurant was busy. That prevented her from thinking too much about yesterday. Their wonderful sex last night. Alan's sweetness in helping her get to a peaceful sleep afterward.

She also wanted to avoid thinking about all her admissions the prior evening about who she'd been, and a lot of what had happened that resulted, ultimately, in her being here this way.

"Hey, you okay?" Tobi had just sashayed up to her near the tables closest to the door, which Kelly had been assigned. The attractive server was grinning and had a stack of menus in her arms.

"I'm fine." The question worried Kelly a little, though. She wondered if the strain she had felt yesterday evening was now imprinted on her face.

"I figured. You look good, well rested, and I'm glad since we're putting together a few tables soon for some of our favorite customers to come in for brunch."

"People from Government Plaza?" Kelly guessed. City council members?

Stan?

And would that mean their security detail would be present, too?

Alan?

"You got it. Our esteemed boss is on the phone now, but she called me into her office first to tell me and put me in charge of getting a prime table for eight ready."

"Great. I'll help." Not that Kelly wanted to get anything ready for Stan. But if nothing else, her ordeal in revealing her innermost turmoil underscored the need within her not only to help her nephew and bring down her brother-in-law, but to do it all as fast as possible.

The last time a city council group had come here for breakfast, Alan had visited the restaurant first and requested that things be set up for them.

That had been when she had met Alan for the first time. And when she had first seen Stan since her recent return to this area.

Now she was an old hand at this, at seeing him and dealing with his obnoxious flirtation at times.

But seeing him was far from her reason for being

here. It was long past the time for her to bring him down and to help Eli.

Would Stan be among the day's diners from the council? Would Paul be with him, too? Would she be able to do anything helpful?

Since the place was busy and they didn't want to irritate any existing customers, she and Tobi enlisted strong and sweet Lang's help, too, and in between taking other orders and serving food, they managed to pull a couple of tables together in the corner and get them set up as though it would be a meal for royalty.

Or at least the closest thing to royal accommodations here at the Haven. A royal court with one member whom Kelly intended to dispose of. Legally, of course.

As they finished setting the table, Ella appeared in the dining room. She examined what they had been doing.

Her boss's aqua dress today was similar in style to the one Kelly had worn to her pseudo-interview at the Blue View yesterday, and glancing at it made her feel a bit guilty. She just hoped Ella never learned of her apparent, although not actual, disloyalty.

"Good job," Ella said, and this was one of the times she sounded as if she meant what she said. "I gather from the phone call I was just on that a few council members intend to hold a brief meeting here over breakfast. They're working on some plans, maybe something to do with another large meeting that we might be able to cater. You know what that means." Her hazel eyes looked first at Kelly, then at each of her nearby colleagues in a manner that made it clear what she wanted. They all had to act in a completely efficient and caring manner, and make their diners truly feel like welcome guests who would want to experience that kind of customer service again and again.

And thereby encourage them to have the Haven cater whatever their next big shindig was intended to be.

Alan wasn't surprised that he, Dodd and Jorge were told by Nevil to accompany the small party of council members to the Haven for brunch in order to provide security to the group. What did surprise him, however, was who that party consisted of.

Among them were Council President Regina Joralli, plus council members Stan Grodon and Susan Arviss, among a couple of others. No one unusual there.

But with them was Grodon's aide, Paul Tirths. He appeared to be fully back on duty helping Grodon, but was he, the only non-council member, there for another reason, as well?

Alan tried to find a moment to sneak into a private corner long enough to text Kelly to alert her. But by the time he was enlisted, there was no way he could branch off to be alone.

The whole group was walking there, and that included the security team.

Nor was there a subtle way for him to impose himself into the middle of the group to eavesdrop on Stan and his assistant, or on anyone else for that matter. The security team was instructed to drop back and remain subtly behind them, to be there if needed but virtually invisible if they weren't.

The early October day was crisp and a bit cool, which felt good since they were pretty much all dressed in business suits. At least Alan felt comfortable as they strode along Main and away from Pacific. They soon turned onto Wallace, and quickly reached the Haven.

Peering in through the large windows, he saw that the place was busy, as usual. But he wasn't only scanning the restaurant for customers. He looked for Kelly, as well.

It was too late to warn her about who was coming, but even so, he wanted to talk to her.

To help protect her identity if Tirths was more likely to recognize who she was.

With his security colleagues, he followed the group of mostly politicos inside. Ella stood there as if awaiting the group, dressed as professionally as this crowd who'd just entered. She was apparently waiting for them, since she motioned for them to follow her among the filled seats in the place to the tables pushed together and set up in the back.

As the council members and Tirths all settled into seats, Alan had to bite his tongue to keep from smiling when Ella said to the council president, Regina, "You are all so very welcome here. But you already know that. I've heard rumors you're planning some kind of large event, and you also know we'll do anything to help you out—even close the place for an evening, if that works best for you."

Regina Joralli, always all business, nevertheless offered a smile, lighting up her fiftysomething face in a way Alan had rarely seen. "I appreciate that, Ella," she said. "But unfortunately it's an afternoon event, and our plans are nearly already complete. We're reserving another venue."

Alan watched Ella's face fall. "Of course," she said.

"But you know we love this place," Regina said hastily. "Why else would we be here now? And you can be sure we'll be back, and also ask you to cater some future events we schedule at the plaza."

Ella looked slightly less sad as she said, "Thank you." She quickly turned, as if to get as far from the group as possible. Alan wondered if she was prone to taking it out on her employees when they didn't get business she was expecting. He hoped not, especially since he saw Kelly and a couple of others approaching from the kitchen just then.

He watched her. He managed to catch her eye, and nodded his head slightly in the direction of where Paul Tirths had taken his seat at the table.

Kelly's eyes widened, but only for an instant. She gave a tiny nod, as if letting him know she got what he was silently saying. Her expression first grew grim, but then she pasted on a smile that he figured was not a Shereen Alsop smile, but one she was trained to use as Kelly Ladd.

That made him want to smile more, too. Kelly was one smart lady, no matter what identity she used.

Now, would her slipping into Tirths's presence help them achieve the goals they had?

That remained to be seen.

Yes, Paul was here. With Stan.

Alan had come, too, of course, and Kelly couldn't have been happier to see him. He had already gestured to her in an appropriately subtle manner, calling attention to the potential elephant in the room. She would have seen Paul anyway, but she appreciated Alan's form of a heads-up.

His presence would hopefully keep her grounded,

ready to do what was professionally necessary to get the goods on Stan, even though that was Alan's job and not hers.

She also hoped having him here would help her keep her mind on the present, not the past.

But the past was still there. And though Stan hadn't recognized her, would Paul?

Everyone from their group who was here had come from the plaza. Dora wasn't among them. This appeared to be all city business, or at least this group might want it to look that way, even with Paul along. He was a city employee, after all, even though he wasn't a council member.

But what did Stan want him to do?

Kelly knew what she wanted to do, so she made herself smile as she withdrew her notepad and pen from her pocket. Ella stood off to the side of the table, not appearing especially happy, and Kelly wondered why. In any event, her boss nodded toward her, and presumably also toward Tobi and Lang. She apparently wanted them to start taking the group's orders.

Kelly nodded back and headed to the end of the table where Stan and Paul sat. She didn't look toward Alan to see if he approved. Even if he didn't, she would still take the orders of those men. They were less likely to look at her if she was behind them, and she would be better able to eavesdrop if she was near them. That was the end of any unspoken debate, for her at least.

Tobi and Lang moved at the same time, as if they were all in sync—and in a way they were.

As she neared Stan and Paul, she saw they were talking to each other, but she couldn't hear what they were saying—which made her want to know what it was even more. She bent down, holding out her pad and pen as if she just wanted to take their orders.

"...get everyone to come," Stan was saying. "It can only help 'em reach agreement on the funding."

"Of course," Paul said. "It'll work better if there are no holdouts, so it's worth it to pay for lunch for everyone—including those at my level."

Kelly didn't know exactly what they were discussing, but she figured it was the upcoming event Ella had mentioned.

Stan glanced toward her then. "Hey, gorgeous, I didn't know you were there." When he reached out as if he wanted to touch her—possibly her breast, which wasn't outside his potential grasp—Kelly stood up quickly and forced herself to smile.

"May I take your orders, gentlemen?" She added a sensual tone to her voice, even though it made her want to gag. But she needed to keep Stan interested—and oblivious to who she was.

"Sure, I'm ready to order," he said. "How about you, Paul?"

Kelly held her breath as Paul glanced toward her, using all she had been taught to exemplify her new persona. He gave her a once-over and grinned as if he, too, found her interesting, which continued to make her feel all squeamish and uncomfortable inside. "Sure, I'm ready, babe." His smile at her just then was lecherous.

But he didn't appear to recognize her, and that was what was most important.

She wished she could say something to him. Slap him or kick him where it hurt for turning against her the way he had.

And here he was, still buddies with Stan, whom Paul

had said had killed his wife. Then Paul had denied ever saying such a heinous thing, let alone giving Shereen proof that she could deliver to the authorities. Nor had he given her proof of who had then started trying to harm Shereen.

"Who's first?" she forced herself to ask, despite having the urge to do something retaliatory to Paul. She said it that way on purpose, knowing they could choose to take those words as suggestive. And they did, at least somewhat, elbowing each other and making some slightly off-color comments. But they finally ordered their sandwiches, and Kelly headed for the kitchen, despite wanting to stay and eavesdrop some more.

Tobi and Lang had beaten her, but she was glad to let them place their customers' orders first. It gave her a good reason just to stand there and breathe and restore her sense of self—as Kelly.

Too bad she couldn't just stay near them and listen. Or figure out some small measure of retaliation that she could take here against Paul.

But after she placed their orders and returned with their soft drinks, she did overhear some of the general conversation at the table. She also saw Alan close by, appearing as if he was aware and on guard and doing his protective security thing. He caught her eye briefly, gave a quick wink and remained there listening.

What he heard must be the same as what Kelly had heard. The city council, with the approval of the mayor, was about to hold a massive event for government employees and local businesspeople, an event at which they would ask those people what they hoped to gain in the next year that would help their businesses as well as Blue Haven.

It was going to be held at the much more expensive Blue View, which told Kelly what she expected to hear. They weren't skimping financially on this event.

Everyone who was anyone would attend and speak their minds—possibly with their hands out. It would occur in the afternoon, two days from now.

As part of his security mission, Alan would undoubtedly be expected to attend, so Kelly would be able to hear at least some of what went on from him later.

And as she stood there, an idea began to percolate in her mind.

Chapter 19

Kelly continued mulling over the idea she had had at the Haven. It wasn't a new idea. Not at all. Just a potentially more feasible way to attempt to extract vital information, now that her mind-set, and circumstances, would allow her to do it.

Following through might not have the kind of positive result she craved, of course. It might not work at all. If it worked only partially, she could wind up feeling even worse, especially if it didn't lead to a new way to attempt to help Eli. But she had to try. She'd been unable to do it before she had fled here as Shereen, but now a rare opportunity appeared to be presenting itself.

She didn't tell Alan what she had in mind. Kelly wasn't sure he was convinced, but she had told him she needed more space, more alone time to work through the angst that had settled in after divulging so much to him before. He hadn't fought her on it.

She saw him during those days, though. He first popped in at the Haven for breakfast alone on Monday, so she had an opportunity to chat with him while acting as his server.

Did he seem relieved that they had both backed off a bit in terms of their heat and intensity? Kelly hoped so...on one level. On all other levels, though, she incongruously felt hurt.

No matter. It was better if they stayed apart, at least for now. She didn't want to even give him a tiny unintentional hint about the plan she was working on. It was certainly not kosher—and it might even be violating the law.

At the Haven on Tuesday, the morning before the crucial date, she smiled when she saw that the stack of local newspapers had been replenished. That week's edition had just been printed and circulated the day after the brunch when the city council members, and Paul Tirths, had sat here eating and devising their plans for their fund-raising event at the Blue View. It contained an article on the pending event.

The local TV station's news hyped it, too. Everyone who was anyone in Blue Haven's government and business communities was expected to be there, going over plans and ideas for next year.

Kelly figured Stan wasn't the only council member who'd try hard to impress those with funds to toss a bunch toward whoever appeared willing to help their businesses' profitability next year.

For an event like that, security would be needed, so Kelly felt confident Alan would be too busy to interfere with what she was up to.

And now, it was still fairly early in the morning on

Wednesday, the crucial day. Breakfast time. Would Alan come today, too?

The Haven was filling up. "You can handle all the tables from here to the wall, right?" Ella had come up behind Kelly as she'd turned to hurry to the kitchen with an order from the nearest customers. Startled, Kelly turned to look first at Ella, and then at all the tables she was referring to.

There were, in fact, more than she generally had charge of. But she had handled this many before, and she knew she would have no trouble with them.

"Sure," she said, and her boss's tense face softened.

"Good job." Ella turned and walked away through the quickly filling tables.

This time, Kelly allowed herself to enjoy the compliment. She actually was a pretty good server these days—even if she had no intention of remaining a server here in Blue Haven for the long term. In fact, she was nearly ready to be done.

That was one more reason to hope her plan yielded something useful that finally, at a minimum, would help Eli…

"Hi, Kelly," said a familiar deep voice from behind her.

She turned, smiling tentatively as she saw Alan's handsome face looking down at her. If she read his expression correctly, he appeared happy to see her. But was that just part of the cover?

"Hi, Alan. Are you here for breakfast?" She managed to glance around him to see if any of the government group he protected had arrived with him, but she saw no one else.

"A quick one. Do you have any tables available?"

Like, one where you'd be serving, she could tell he was thinking.

"Definitely." She led him through the maze of filled chairs around busy tables to the far wall, where a couple of tables were still unoccupied.

"Thanks," he said warmly. "I'll have some wheat toast and coffee when you get a chance."

"I'll put the order in for you right away."

She headed for the kitchen, where she left the appropriate note for the chefs, then picked up an order she needed to deliver to a table not far from where Alan sat.

She didn't try to fool herself. She was glad he was here, even though it was part of the same old undercover role he was playing—demonstrating some interest in her so it wouldn't arouse anyone's suspicions if they were seen talking to each other.

But was anyone even paying attention to them? She hoped not. Yet she didn't mind playing this game, in case it helped. And also because she felt both pleasure and relief in Alan's presence, though she couldn't tell him what was now at the forefront of her mind.

She headed back into the dining area, her arms loaded with a tray containing omelets and other egg dishes.

"Here you are," she said to the woman who had ordered the Western omelet, then went about setting the rest of the food from the tray in front of the others at the same table.

When she had finally placed all the items down for the customers, she allowed the tray to go a little slack in her hands and turned to head back to the kitchen. Her eyes lit on Alan's for an instant first—but he wasn't looking at her. Instead, he was gazing over her shoulder. She had gotten to know him well enough to be able to interpret his expressions, for the most part, and this one looked blank—the kind of expression he got when he was hiding what he was really feeling. An expression that meant he wasn't happy.

Kelly turned slowly in the direction he was staring and felt her own face grow blank.

Stan Grodon and Paul Tirths had entered the Haven, and with them was Dora Shallner. Ella was showing them to a table at the edge of those where Kelly was serving. They were talking animatedly among themselves. That was probably a good thing. They were unlikely to pay much attention to Kelly, and she would hopefully be able to listen to them.

She gave Alan a glance as she moved past his table toward the kitchen, giving Stan and his group time to look at their menus while she picked up the orders for another table. Alan looked up at her as well, his expression blank enough to tell her he had some concerns. She just shot him a half smile and continued on.

A short while later, after bringing out several pancake orders for another table, Kelly took a deep breath, steadied herself and headed for the table that was now the subject of her concerns.

"Good morning," she said, careful to take her place standing across from Stan, not wanting to be too close to his grasping hands in case Dora's presence wasn't enough to keep him from touching Kelly if he decided he was in the mood to flirt.

"Hi, gorgeous." But after a quick ogle of her, Stan looked quickly toward Dora and gave her a wink.

Dora just shook her head briefly, then turned toward Kelly. "Well, hi, Kelly. I'd just like a single egg, over easy, with rye toast, plus a coffee with cream. It's so good to see you here, and you can consider our visit today a test." The smile she aimed toward Kelly was friendly, yet a bit cool. Kelly figured she was serious—that she considered this visit a test of her capability both as a server, and as a woman who recognized that one of her customers wanted the man who pretended to flirt with her to back off.

Kelly was happy to do both well. She hoped the smile she returned to Dora, and her efficiency after that in asking for their orders, conveyed that.

She felt more than a little uncomfortable, though, when she took Paul's order. She had seen him here before, and had even waited on him. This time, he appeared to actually look at her. But as far as she could tell, he didn't see her as anything but the persona she had adopted here, which was definitely a good thing.

She rushed their orders to the kitchen, then spent what time she could with her back toward the group as she hovered over nearby tables and their occupants, listening, but learning nothing more about the gala planned for that afternoon—other than that all three of them intended to be there.

She couldn't have been happier to see any other customers leave than when this group had eaten and departed. Alan left around the same time, too, after trading further glances with her. They didn't take the time to get together to talk, though.

Kelly wasn't exactly happy about how the day had gone so far—but she had at least learned enough to hope that it would turn out as well as she wished.

Alan wasn't happy. He hadn't had a chance to do more than treat Kelly as a server that morning, enjoying no further conversation. In fact, that was the way things had been between them for the past few days. He wanted to spend more time with her—even time when he was not touching her. They were supposed to be working together, at least as long as she remained here. He had to be sure not to push her back to her other life.

Right now, he was hurrying back toward Government Plaza, where he would spend the next couple of hours on his security detail there, then follow the city council members up to the Blue View.

The streets were busy, the usual midmorning traffic jam in this area well under way. The sidewalk and steps into the plaza were also quite crowded. There seemed to be more people than usual coming and going, including some Alan recognized as secretaries and assistants to the council members. They were most likely preparing for the afternoon's festivities.

Alan, too, hurried up the steps—or at least he hurried as much as he could with the crowds around him. After going through security, he headed down the hall to his office as quickly as he could.

Dodd was there, as were two of their coworkers, Prentice and Jorge. "Did I miss anything important while I was gone?" Alan asked.

"Not much," Dodd said. "Unless you think that the resignation of our fearless leader, Nevil, is important."

"What!" Alan hadn't given much thought to Nevil Hancock, but he'd apparently run the private security company forever. Alan had heard some criticism of him now and then from the council members, but only when he had been eavesdropping, and none of it had sounded like a big deal.

"Yeah." Jorge shook his shaved bald head back and forth. "Rumors are circulating, with more information to come, we've been told."

"Is he around today?"

"Not that I've seen," Prentice said, straightening his tie, which stretched along his large belly, over his shirt.

"But we're under orders to do exactly what we had been planning," Dodd said. The senior security guy shook his head. "That big party our illustrious council is throwing at the Blue View this afternoon? We're in charge of making sure it goes smoothly, at least from the security standpoint. Police Chief Sangler stopped in to confirm it."

Their involvement was, in fact, what Alan had anticipated. He wanted to talk more to Kelly about what he would attempt to do there, but she was working today, and so was he.

He'd get in touch with her after the council shindig, though. Maybe they could grab dinner together. And perhaps more? That sounded good, but mostly he wanted to catch up with her, discuss more concrete ideas at last that they could implement together for getting to the bottom of the Stan situation and protecting Eli.

Yes, he would be in Stan's presence that afternoon, but at a big public to-do like this where he most likely wouldn't get any useful information. But he had developed some good ideas that were workable and quick.

"So who's doing what at the Blue View this afternoon?" Dodd pressed. "Looks like we won't be getting specific orders from our boss."

Not that they really ever did, Alan thought. Maybe it would be better for this group to get a new leader anyway.

For right now, he plunged into the discussion of who would watch the doors, who would take charge of the parking lot and who would unobtrusively patrol the restaurant facility. He hoped for the latter and made that clear, though not the reason for it: wanting to listen to people as much as possible.

In any event, it sounded like he had a boring afternoon ahead of him.

The closer she got to her destination, the more Kelly became excited about the possibilities that could come of her plan. It was her first opportunity since arriving here to give it a try. It had to work.

She was nearly there! At the moment, she was just walking nonchalantly yet carefully along the pavement on this narrow, hedge-lined alleyway behind the homes on the street where Stan and Eli lived now—and where Andi also used to live. Was it wise? Maybe not, but at the moment she didn't care.

She was carrying a bag of sandwiches from the Haven, so if anyone spotted or stopped her she could claim she was trying to deliver some food but had gotten lost.

She'd parked a couple of blocks away, too, so no one would be able to determine where her destination was.

But for now, she could hardly breathe, and that wasn't just because of the rank alley smell of trash and car exhaust trapped here. She was determined, yes—but also nervous. At least she had gotten over her initial fear of even coming by here.

She moved along quietly, walking right up against the bushes to make herself a tiny bit less obvious.

What would be Alan's opinion of what she was up

to? She shouldn't even think about his reaction, since she knew he'd be more than a little peeved. After all, his partner here, his fake love interest, was preparing to break into a house—his target's house—to discover something that might or might not exist. Plus, it was not legal for her, an apparent stranger, to enter a councilman's house uninvited, even though she had once, in her real persona, been related to him. And Alan was all about doing things correctly. And Alan also—

No. Don't think about him at all, she told herself.

Especially not now. She was nearing the break in the hedge that led to the back gate of the Grodon property.

Surely Stan would have changed the lock by now. It had been more than a year since his wife "disappeared"—or, more likely, was murdered by him. If Kelly couldn't get in the easy way, she was prepared to climb over the hedges, since the nearest homes that also backed onto this alley were far enough away that, even if someone was home, the occupants wouldn't be able to see her.

But fortunately, the set of keys she had been given by her sister a few years ago still worked, or at least this one did. She heaved a sigh of relief as she unlocked the gate, then closed it behind her.

She looked up at the rear of the tall, beige stone mansion Andi had once called home. No one would be there now. It was the middle of the afternoon on a Wednesday. Eli would be in school.

And Stan would be at that huge event he'd planned, intending to bring him—and others—lots of prestige... and money.

Despite her fears, this was something Kelly had

hoped to do since returning here, but had never felt comfortable that the house would be empty. Till now.

She glanced around. There were houses on either side, over the tall fence surrounding the place, but they were far enough away that even if someone happened to look out a window, she was unlikely to be seen. That was one good thing about Andi having lived in such an elite neighborhood.

Not that Kelly—Shereen—had ever been jealous of her sister, even when her marriage hadn't looked too awful.

For now, Kelly hurried toward the back of the house. Was she going to be lucky enough that the key she had for that door would work, too?

Kelly had an alternate plan, just in case. Long ago, Andi had shown her younger sister another way to get into the house in an emergency. It involved a window along the right side that led to the basement. The window had no lock, but even if it did now, it was low and easily breakable.

Or so Kelly hoped.

But no need for that! The key she had fit into this lock, too. Was Stan really that confident in his invulnerability? But then, Andi had made it clear, way back when, that Shereen should never even hint to Stan that she had a way into their precious home, not even in an emergency. And no one else would ever have been provided with keys, except perhaps Eli now that he was older. They used to have, and possibly still had, a cleaning service, but its employees had only ever come before Stan left for work, and he had always returned home at lunchtime on those days to make sure everything was locked up.

In moments, Kelly was through the back door and inside the amazing kitchen, with its steel appliances, that was much nicer than the one at the Haven. And she knew where to head to search for anything Andi might have left that expressed her concerns about Stan.

The plan she'd barely dared to consider once she'd come to Blue Haven just might be coming to fruition after all.

Yes, Shereen had told the authorities about the locations she would now check out. But there'd been some lack of communication—possibly because of who Stan was. As far as Shereen had ever known, Stan and his lawyer had been around the house when it had been the subject of an official search, and nothing had been found.

But maybe everything had already been destroyed by Stan by that time.

But just in case, Kelly was going to head for the area beneath the staircase to the second floor, then she would look—

Wait! She heard a noise toward the front of the house. Stan had never been one to have pets, so it wasn't likely to be a dog or cat that had heard her.

And now she heard footsteps. She wasn't alone. Surely Stan hadn't come back here now, instead of attending his party. But who—

Kelly wasn't about to hurry that way to find out. Instead, she planted herself between the tall refrigerator and the door to the basement. If she'd had time, she would have hurried down the basement steps, but for now she just waited.

For whom?

And what was going to happen next?

Chapter 20

Whoever it was had headed in her direction. Kelly could hear the footsteps coming down the hall toward the kitchen.

Had she been seen after all? She still held the bag with food in it, but that would have really only worked if she was outside. She could hardly claim she had broken into the house to leave sandwiches in the kitchen.

She wanted to laugh at the absurdity of that excuse, at the same time as she felt an urge to cry.

What if it was Stan here after all? He would have no scruples at all about killing her the way he had undoubtedly done to Andi, and no one knew she was here.

She should have told Alan what she was up to. She—

The person entered the kitchen. The footsteps sounded different on the tile floor here from how they'd sounded on the wood outside.

Maybe whoever it was wouldn't come this far. Maybe she could—

"Hey!" It was Eli's voice. Kelly almost breathed a sigh of relief. Almost. She was a stranger to him, not his aunt. And whoever she was, she shouldn't be here. "Is someone here?"

How would he know? She'd closed the door behind her. But he must have heard her come in.

Then she saw that a dish towel hung limply from the indoor sill of the window right by the door, nearly ready to fall. It was fairly large. Had it been hooked partly over the doorknob?

If so, why?

Maybe young Eli played this trick so he would know if he was alone when he played hooky from school. Because that was apparently what he was doing.

What should she do?

He would most likely come this way soon. She didn't want to scare him, but simply staying still was just as likely to frighten him as waiting till he spotted her here. So she took a step out from behind the fridge. "Hello, Eli," she said in a tone that had once been natural to her, before she'd had her identity changed. Or she hoped it sounded natural. It had been a while since she had spoken in that voice.

Her nephew was dressed in a black T-shirt over jeans. He looked so much like his mother, with straight brown hair, deep brown eyes that glowered even as his mouth edged open in apparent fear, soft yet attractive facial features and a lean body.

"Who are you? What are you doing here?" As Kelly opened her mouth, hoping that a great way to tell him who she was would suddenly come to her, he started looking her up and down. "You...you don't look like my aunt Shereen, but you just sounded like her. And there's something... Who are you?" he repeated. He looked both terrified and intrigued.

"You're right," she said quietly. "I'm Aunt Shereen. I had to leave here to protect myself after...after your mother disappeared. I had to make myself look different. But I'm back because I was worried about you."

"Yeah, sure." His tone was harsh. "Are you a friend of my father's? What are you trying to do?"

Kelly had known this wouldn't be easy, but she pressed on. "I came here because I saw you on some social media sites looking...well, looking sad again. And more. And I couldn't let..." She stopped, but only for a moment. "Look, let's go sit down and I'll tell you about it."

The affair at the Blue View was huge. Alan hadn't been in town long enough to meet, or even see, most of Blue Haven's muckety-mucks, but he expected that everyone he saw here in their big smiles and expensive finery was among them—either them or their minions.

Many milled around with drinks in their hands, since the meal had yet to be served. Some stood near the large windows, looking out at the gorgeous and vast view.

Alan stood near the door to the kitchen, watching the crowd. He wished Kelly were here with him, and not as a server. But it was probably better that she not be present. She almost certainly wouldn't be recognized, but why waste her time, too?

Alan couldn't get near enough to Stan, who stood among the tables, to eavesdrop on his conversations with Jerome Baranka and Dora Shallner, whom he was hanging out with, but he doubted anything they were saying would be of much assistance to reaching his goal anyway.

So, for now, he just watched.

And he became very interested when Stan apparently got a call, since he reached into his coat pocket and extracted his phone. He looked at the screen first, then moved toward the window to talk.

His expression turned dark. In moments, after hanging up, he made his way through the crowd, headed not back to those he had been speaking with, but toward where Paul Tirths stood with some other assistants from Government Plaza.

They talked for only a moment. Paul nodded, and he headed for the door as Stan, still appearing miffed, returned to Baranka and Dora.

The whole thing left Alan wondering what that was about.

And boy, did he have an urge to follow Paul.

They were sitting on the plush antique sofa in the living room. Eli still looked at Kelly as if she was a stranger he didn't trust.

She understood that. Even if a tiny part of him thought she was his aunt, she had betrayed him before by running away. And now, no matter what she said, he might have a hard time believing she had come back to help him.

She sat back on the sofa with her right leg crossed over the left one. It was a pose that she had struck often back when she was only Shereen. She had changed all of those habits when she had assumed her new identity.

Eli still looked dubious but, unless it was her imagination, maybe a little less so than before.

"Here's the thing."

That was a phrase she had also used often as Shereen, one that, when she started using it around the ID Division at first, she had been told to drop. Eli's light eyebrows lifted at that.

The ID Division. Should she tell her nephew about that? Not now. She'd already betrayed them by coming here—as Alan never let her forget. But describing their existence and what they were? No, she wouldn't do that.

If nothing else, she would protect those who had protected her—and she would do nothing to jeopardize Alan. If only he were with her now...well, if she succeeded in this mission, he would be the third to know about it, after Eli and herself.

She continued. "I didn't think anyone would be home today, and I know where your mom used to keep some of the documents and things that we inherited when our parents, your grandparents, passed away. She'd told me not only their location, but that she kept some other important stuff there, as well. When the police were looking into your mother's disappearance, I told the investigators, but I heard that your dad and his lawyer followed them around, and—well, with your dad being such an important personality around here, maybe the authorities were intimidated enough to take shortcuts, and never checked the places I mentioned. I just figured that while I was in town I'd check them out."

"Like that hidden area under the steps upstairs?" A sardonic look appeared on Eli's young face.

"Yes." But Kelly felt her insides fall. If he knew about it, then Stan would, too. That was where Kelly had assumed Andi had hidden the concerns about her personal and professional life that she'd hinted about documenting. The detectives, promising they would reveal nothing to the man they were investigating, had claimed they hadn't found anything, but Kelly had wanted to look anyway. She had to ask, "Is there anything there?"

"No. Not now. But—" Now Eli's expression grew triumphant, if Kelly was reading him correctly. "I found something that tells what she was thinking. That's why my dad has been mad at me."

"Really?" Kelly found herself standing, grinning down at her nephew. But then she realized there could be problems. "Does your dad have it?"

"No. I've been able to hide it, and it's driving him crazy."

Crazy enough to strike his son, Kelly thought, and possibly more.

That suggested that, whatever it was, it might be the answer to bringing Stan down.

He had to be realistic. Alan knew that. He had a job to do here, at the Blue View. Two jobs. His cover was to stay here and make sure all went smoothly from a security perspective with all of the town's top politicians.

Then there was his real job—and he was in the presence of his main target.

So for the moment he remained in the restaurant. He had gotten the assignment to patrol inside, which was not too bad considering the posh facilities and the people who were there.

Yes, there was a police presence, too, but their assignment was to keep an eye on the whole place and make sure nothing went wrong from a regular police patrol perspective.

Private security here was to blend in and also make sure nothing went wrong and nothing happened to make the attending city council members and their business associates unhappy.

Theoretically, that would gave Alan more opportunity to stake out Stan Grodon and his cronies, eavesdrop on them, hopefully learn something new.

That hadn't happened yet.

And he hadn't been close enough to hear Stan talking with the now-absent Paul. This remained on Alan's mind, even as he smiled and maneuvered through the crowd of people holding glasses of alcoholic beverages and chattering about inanities, from all he could tell.

Where was Paul?

Should he have followed him?

What was he up to?

"So tell me about this mysterious thing your dad is after." Kelly tried to keep her voice light as she sat back on the couch holding a glass of water. Eli had insisted on getting them something to drink before they talked. She knew it was just procrastination, but that had been fine with her...temporarily.

Still, would this revelation from Eli be the key to what had happened to Andi?

Why else would Stan brutalize his son over it? Although it could just be the SOB's excuse...

"It's Mom's tablet." Eli's young face suddenly seemed a lot older as it assumed a dual look of both guilt and defiance. He, too, remained seated on the sofa, but his posture appeared stiff, as if he held himself there to keep from fleeing.

Which only made Kelly feel worse. But she had to press, especially because she was suddenly filled with an optimism she hadn't felt since...well, since Andi had disappeared.

Andi's tablet could be a really big clue. She had used one in her real estate transactions, for one thing. Nothing she'd included about her deals was likely to provide any indication of what had happened to her, but maybe some more detail about the dispute between her company and Baranka's, and Stan's interference in it, could shed a light on it.

And the fact that it hadn't been found during the investigation into her disappearance? That made Kelly even more curious about its contents, and Stan apparently felt the same way.

"I see," Kelly said to Eli in a normal conversational tone, her mind scrambling to determine how best to play this. She had to reassure him she was on his side. And yet she sought possible possession of something he clearly considered important. "Any idea why your dad wants it so much?"

"Yeah." Eli glared at her as if challenging her to push him—figuratively and literally, as his father had undoubtedly done.

Kelly leaned forward. "I understand that you have good reason not to trust me," she said quietly, not taking her eyes from his. "I disappeared when you needed me most. But I think you were old enough even then to understand that I felt...well, threatened. Things kept happening to me after your mother disappeared, and even so, I didn't stop looking for her, and pushing the authorities to find her, too. I didn't want to give up, but getting killed wouldn't help me to learn the truth, nor would it allow me to help you."

"You thought my dad was trying to kill you." His tone didn't sound accusatory, just realistic. "I figured that at the time. And I wasn't much younger than I am now, so don't try to play that card on me. That's one thing my dad does, and he knows I hate it."

There was so much in what he had just said that she wanted him to elaborate on—and that made her ache to scoot over to his side of the couch and hug him.

"Okay," she said. "You're a teenager now, but you weren't then." She hadn't been around for his thirteenth birthday…and she also hadn't been sure she would ever be with him again for any other birthdays.

She still wasn't.

"You were smart beyond your years even then. And if I could have found a way to bring you with me and keep you safe, I would have. But I figured that, even if your dad had killed your mom, he loved you and wouldn't hurt you, no matter what he thought of me."

"Yeah, when we first couldn't find Mom, he kept acting all sad around me, said she'd run away, that kind of thing. And anyone who thought he'd done something to her—like you—well, you were all wrong. That's what he said." Eli's voice was low and practically a monotone, and he looked down at his hands clasped together in his lap. "I wanted to believe him. I did believe him. Until…well, I started worrying when he cleaned out all of Mom's things, although when I mentioned it to Cal's mom she just said it was probably because my dad was grieving so much that he wanted to try to put everything behind him." Eli looked up at Kelly as if searching for her opinion on her face.

"Some people do that," she agreed, without stating the reasons Stan had probably wanted to get rid of all of Andi's belongings—even those that had belonged to her family, those that should now be Shereen's.

"I got it, even tried to help him, but he didn't want my help, which made me feel even worse. And then... well, I started removing some stuff right after school, before Dad got home. I took it over to Cal's, and he didn't tell his mom but helped me hide it in a big box he kept under his bed."

The idea excited Kelly. What was there? Anything that might lead to answers about what had happened to her sister? But she knew she had to play this cool and not upset Eli. "That was a good idea," she said simply.

"I figure you'll want to take a look at it, won't you?" His expression had turned as wry as an adult's, and Kelly grinned as she nodded.

"And the tablet?" she asked. "Where was it? And where is it now?"

"It wasn't in her things under the stairs, so it's not your old family stuff." Eli's voice was chilly now. "The thing is...well, she'd hidden it in the bureau in my room, in a padded envelope in a drawer that had some clothes I hadn't grown into yet...then."

Smart lady, Kelly thought. But then, her sister had always been smart. Except the bit about marrying Stan.

"So now that you're a little older, and bigger, you found it," she stated to her nephew, not making it a question.

"Yep. With all that had happened, I wanted to look at it without my dad knowing, so I went through it on afternoons when I got home early. It was mostly boring real estate stuff in those computer files, but—" Eli stood up and was suddenly right in front of Kelly. "She was scared, Aunt Shereen. She didn't tell anyone, I don't think, but those files…they were almost like a diary, and she kept notes about how my dad was against her in some real estate stuff and was going to kill her if she didn't let him get his own way. She also…she bought a cabin way up in the mountains, it said, where she was going to take me and run away if things got any worse."

Well, they'd gotten a whole lot worse, Kelly thought, also standing and hugging Eli close against her as the boy began to cry. Tears came to her eyes, too.

Could Andi have run away to that cabin?

If so, why had no one seen her since then? Was she like Shereen, undercover with a new identity?

Where was Andi now?

"Did you tell your dad about the tablet?" she asked, assuming he had, since his father had started abusing him.

"No, but—well, I got scared and yelled at him about the way he'd acted with my mom, and he asked me what I found. I just said it was something important."

Then Stan had made an assumption, and Eli hadn't denied finding something. Even if Stan didn't know what it was, he would undoubtedly do a lot to retrieve it—even hurt his own son.

"We need to turn that tablet over to the authorities, Eli," Kelly said firmly.

"No."

"But—"

"They'll just destroy it. All the cops and everyone

here in town are my dad's friends, or at least they want to impress him."

She knew Eli was a smart kid, but this observation was not only very true, it was also something an adult might not even recognize.

There was an answer, though. A perfect answer. "Eli, you've met that nice security guy Alan. He has a different agenda from the regular police and others." Not that she could explain what it was, or how she knew... "You can give him the tablet, and—"

"You can give me the tablet," a gruff male voice said suddenly.

Eli cried "No!" and ran to the far side of the room. As Kelly gasped, she turned to the door into the living room, expecting to see Stan there. Instead, it was Paul Tirths.

Kelly swallowed hard, struggling to come up with a story that she could sell to Paul—about who she was now, not who she used to be. "Oh, hello," she said. "I met Eli at Government Plaza, and he called the Haven Restaurant where I worked and asked me to bring him a sandwich. He's such a nice young man that I—"

"Shove it, Shereen." Paul was staring straight at her. "I don't know why you look that way, but I was listening for a while." He turned to Eli. "Your school called your dad and said you left without permission. He sent me to find you. Good thing I did. Now, give me that tablet."

Walking toward the entrance to the room, Kelly planted herself in front of Paul. "Please, Paul," she said, using her old voice, the one from before the coaching she had undergone. "You used to be on my side. You understood. We may have a way to learn the truth now, even have evidence. You—"

"You don't need to know my reasons, Shereen, but I'm on Stan's side now. In fact, he's on his way here." He sidestepped her and faced the cowering Eli. "Give me that tablet, kid. I'm going to tell your dad about it anyway, and he'll get it from you no matter what. If you volunteer it, things will be a lot easier on you."

"You can't promise that!" Kelly yelled. "Eli, don't listen to him."

"I won't." The boy sounded firm and belligerent. "I'm not telling you where it is."

Paul moved suddenly, and Kelly felt his arm go tightly around her throat.

"If you want your aunt to live, kid, go get that tablet."

Chapter 21

Alan had been across the room listening to Council-woman Arviss promote her student internship program to a couple of other council members—and keeping an eye on the rest of the room—when he noticed Stan pull his phone from his pocket and look at it, presumably reading a text message.

His eyes widened, then narrowed, or at least that was what Alan thought he saw from this distance.

Stan said something to the group of business executives around him, smiled, waved—and started toward the restaurant door.

He was leaving? This was his event...or maybe he just needed to go outside for something.

Alan had to find out.

It was his turn to smile and nod as he headed through the crowded restaurant, between the filled seats at the tables and the groups of people that had formed in areas between those tables. Fortunately, he spotted Dodd in the direction he was going. Dodd had also gotten one of the plum assignments of the afternoon—to stay inside the restaurant and ensure the crowd's security. Alan headed toward him first.

"Sorry, got a personal matter to attend to," he told his more senior colleague. "Not sure what my timing will be, but I'll try to come back as soon as possible."

"Personal—as in that luscious Kelly?" Dodd's suggestive smile would have made Alan want to slug him—if he'd had the time.

The other problem was that he was afraid the situation did involve Kelly. That was just a hunch. Or maybe it was really a fear, since she wasn't with him. Whatever Stan was doing surely had nothing to do with her. It couldn't.

But he had to find out for sure, and learn what Stan Grodon might be up to.

"That's my business," Alan said, but he made himself smile back at Dodd and stick a suggestive leer on his face just so his friend wouldn't ask more questions.

Then he made his way out the door—just in time to see a valet turn Stan's expensive silver sedan over to him.

Alan's own car wasn't far from the restaurant entry, but he was concerned he'd lose Stan before he could start to follow him. He ran to his car and, once inside, began heading down the narrow mountainous road after him.

But Stan was already too far away. By the time Alan reached the bottom of the hill, he could not tell where Stan's car had gone.

Alan knew of a couple of possibilities, at least. He first drove in the direction of downtown, toward Government Plaza. He took shortcuts that should have led him to Stan's car before he arrived…assuming that was where the man was headed.

In the meantime, he tried calling Kelly…just because. Her phone went straight to voice mail.

Did that mean Alan's ridiculous initial concern was valid—that this had something to do with her after all?

He hoped not, yet his instincts told him she was in trouble.

He didn't see Stan's car on his way to the plaza, nor did he see it in the parking facilities there. He slammed the steering wheel with his hand.

He had to find Stan. Better yet, he had to find Kelly and make sure she was all right.

After parking along the street outside the plaza, he again tried calling her—and again was directed straight to voice mail. What was he going to do now?

His phone rang, and he quickly looked at it. Could it be Kelly? No, it was a strange phone number.

"Hello?" he said, hating to take the time to answer. He intended to head to Stan's home, in case he could find the councilman there.

"Hello, is this Alan?" said a young-sounding male voice. "This is Eli Grodon."

Alan's heart pounded as questions surged through his mind. "Yes," he said. "This is Alan Correy. How are you, Eli?"

Why would Eli be calling him? How had he gotten Alan's phone number?

Where was Kelly? Was she all right?

"I'm not doing great," Eli said. "Can you come to my house now? I really need to talk to you."

"Where are we going?" Kelly asked again as loudly as she could, hating how her voice sounded so raspy and scared.

But she had been tied up and tossed onto the floor of the backseat of the luxurious sedan Stan drove—another sign of his ill-gotten wealth.

"I told you before," Stan snapped from the front seat. He turned the wheel fast enough that Kelly's head hit the floor. Her neck, and much of the rest of her body, were already sore from lying at this angle. But she'd had no choice except to let him truss her up this way and toss her into his car, which he had parked in his garage. He had a gun. He had threatened her—and Eli.

No one had seen what he had done to her. No neighbor, at least.

Paul had, of course. And so had Eli.

Eli. He was the reason Kelly hadn't tried—much—to fight Stan. Paul was now in charge of him.

Stan had said he would be home soon, without Eli's aunt. If Eli was a good boy and listened to Paul, he could be sure that Kelly would remain okay. If he didn't…well, Stan didn't tell his son what might happen.

Kelly knew that the chances she would come out of this alive were slim to none. But Stan had intimated that Shereen was going to go visit Eli's mother.

Would he take her to wherever he had hidden Andi's body?

If so, and if Kelly died, too, she would at least gain

that little bit of knowledge. But she wanted so badly to let other people know...

Stan turned his radio on and began listening to some shrieking operatic music, obviously not wanting to talk to Kelly, or even listen if she tried again to say something.

Fortunately, the ride had mostly been smooth so far. Kelly struggled some more with the ropes that bound her arms, but again it was to no avail.

If only she could talk to Alan, communicate with him some way, but that was impossible. One of the first things Stan had done when he entered his home and aimed that gun at her was to have Paul grab her purse, which held her cell phone.

She wanted to tell Alan where she was so he could save her.

And if that was impossible, she at least wanted to tell him goodbye...

The smoothness of the ride suddenly changed. The engine grew louder, its sound less masked by the shrieking radio music.

Kelly was pressed against the backseat. The road was clearly sloping upward.

Into the mountains?

To Andi's cabin?

Kelly had realized, after Eli had mentioned it, that the cabin could have become a refuge for Andi—or her last resting place, if Stan had learned about it.

Was he driving her there now so she would join her sister in life...or death? All Stan had told her before about their destination was that it would answer some of Kelly's questions so that maybe, at last, she would shut up.

* * *

Alan parked at the curb several houses away from Stan Grodon's home. He wasn't sure what he would find there, why Eli had called him. How he had called him—how he'd gotten his phone number.

Without answers to these questions, he had to treat this situation like an operation in which he would be using all of his official training and intuition to help the kid.

And Kelly? She had to be involved in this, too, at least in some manner.

He could only hope that she was still okay.

He exited his car, then stayed close to the fences at the outer perimeters of the neighbors' property, in case Stan had come home and Eli had called Alan because he was in danger.

He didn't see Stan's car, but there was an alleyway behind the place lined with tall fences, and presumably a driveway there leading into a garage.

Another tall wooden fence ran along the sidewalk, but Alan could see the upper story of the large, attractive beige home that was Stan's and his son's—and that was also once his missing wife's.

Alan kept his cell phone in his left hand, leaving his right hand free to reach toward the holster hidden beneath his shirt if he needed to draw his weapon. When he got to the gate in the critical fence, he assumed it would be locked, but was surprised when it opened for him with no trouble.

His mind had already devised a premise for showing up here if he was confronted by Stan. As part of the security team for the city council, he wanted to make sure that the important member who'd left the big party was okay. It was a bit flimsy, yes, but it was the best thing he could come up with.

Since he was going to use that story if he had to, he decided not to walk around the house to scope it out first. Besides, getting inside quickly might be imperative.

He walked up the path to the porch steps, climbed them and rang the doorbell.

He listened but heard nothing inside. Had Stan come here, retrieved his son, then left?

Was young Eli all right?

Alan thought he discerned some shuffling footsteps, then the ornate front door opened. Eli stood there.

"I'm glad you're here." The kid's face was ashen. "Come in, okay?"

"Of course." Alan crossed the threshold, following Eli into the entry hall.

The kid closed the door behind them. He wore a black T-shirt over jeans, plus athletic shoes—the outfit he had worn to school?

Why was he here instead of there?

"Eli, I'd really like to know—"

"Please, come in here." The kid's tone sounded urgent, so Alan obeyed. Eli led him into the kitchen.

No one else was there. Where was his father?

Alan started to ask, but Eli, standing right in front of him by a long tile counter, turned and looked up at him with scared brown eyes, light eyebrows drawn into a stricken curve. "My aunt said I could trust you," he said in a soft, scared voice.

His aunt? Then Kelly/Shereen had identified herself to him? When? Where?

Once again Alan opened his mouth to start asking questions, but Eli continued talking, looking down at his feet. "I don't understand it all. But my dad—I think he did something to my mom. My aunt ran away, and then she came back looking different but said she wanted to help me."

"Yes, she does," Alan put in gently, grasping for something to say to make the kid get to the point faster—like, what was going on now.

"She came here before. You know?" He looked up at Alan, who nodded to encourage Eli to continue despite not having been aware of it. "She said I should trust you," he repeated, seeming to study Alan's face as if he could somehow read in it whether that could be true. "I... I don't know, but—"

"I understand that it must be hard to trust anybody right now with all that's been going on. I know you trust Councilwoman Arviss, but she doesn't know the background stuff you're worrying about. And—"

Alan heard a noise, some kind of *thump* from somewhere in the house. He froze for a second, then glared at Eli. "Is someone else here?"

Once more the boy looked down, this time as he nodded. "I... I told Mr. Tirths that the tablet my dad wants is under the steps. He went there to look, and I was able to push him and lock him in there."

Alan couldn't help a brief smile, so he was glad Eli wasn't looking directly at him.

"I see," he said. "Where's that tablet now? And where's your dad?"

"He...he told me I'd better give Mr. Tirths the tablet if I wanted to see my aunt alive again. He's taking her to see my mom, only...only I think my mom's dead."

Alan felt his heart stop beating for a moment. "And

where is this?" He tried not to yell, to shake the kid, but searched for patience...even though he knew that every moment he didn't start off after Stan Grodon and Kelly meant she could be another moment closer to death.

"See, my mom was scared of my dad, and she wrote stuff on that tablet that she didn't want him to see. Then she hid it so he wouldn't find it. Some of the stuff on it says she bought a cabin up in the mountains where she wanted to take me someday to keep us both safe. But the way my dad's been talking about it, I think he took my mom up there and killed her." His voice broke, and he again looked up at Alan.

Pity shot through Alan. This poor kid. How long had he suspected...or known? "And your dad was aware you knew about it," he said gently.

"At first he acted like he missed Mom, too, but then he started asking me questions that told me he wondered what I knew. He didn't know at first that I'd found Mom's tablet and all the stuff she'd put on there."

"Including the location of the cabin."

Eli nodded solemnly. "I'll go get the tablet for you, Mr. Correy. Only... I really can trust you, can't I?"

Alan nodded emphatically. "And you can trust that I'll do my damnedest to go save your aunt," he told the kid.

A few minutes later Alan had the tablet in his possession—which was possibly the very evidence the ID Division was after—as he drove like a maniac toward the cabin at the address he'd found on the tablet that Eli had in fact given him.

He also had Kelly's cell phone. She'd been forced to hand her purse to Paul, Eli said, but the kid had grabbed it away when he shoved the guy under the steps, and her phone had been in it, apparently turned off by Paul. Eli had turned it back on, and that was how he had gotten Alan's phone number.

Alan had already called not only his security company colleagues but also Chief Sangler of the local cops, filling him in on the situation briefly—and letting him know that someone who had conspired with Councilman Grodon in the apparent murder of his wife was locked under some stairs in the councilman's house.

He had ordered Eli to go back to school, since Councilwoman Arviss, his closest adult friend here, was at the festivities up at the Blue View. The kid might be in trouble at school, but a lot of people would be around to protect him if Tirths somehow escaped before the cops came.

And now, Alan could only hope that he arrived at that cabin in time to save Kelly. Good thing he had the information from the tablet plus his GPS to tell him how to get to the cabin in this unknown wilderness.

But would he get there fast enough?

Chapter 22

The cabin was as rustic as anything Kelly had ever seen—there were log walls with no insulation over them, uneven wooden floors, a large cot in one corner and a kitchen that consisted of a metal sink, a portable refrigerator, a propane stove and some enclosed cabinets that might—or might not—contain cooking appliances and serving ware.

Not that she could see much of it. At least she was sitting up now. Stan had half led, half dragged her in from the car once he'd parked beneath the trees surrounding the place. Kelly was stiff, so any kind of movement was a little painful. She saw another door in the far wall, which she presumed led to a bathroom. Or maybe it was a rear exit leading to the outhouse.

Maybe…

"It's been a long ride," she told Stan. "I need to use the restroom."

"Sure," he said with a smirk. "Right there." He pointed toward the door in question. "And in case you're wondering, the room has windows, but they're locked."

He did at least untie her and push her toward the room that was her goal. Could she somehow lock the door and simply stay there till...till what? Till her hero Alan somehow learned where she was and showed up here to save her?

Yeah, right.

She did take her time in the room—at least it had adequate facilities—and rinsed her hands, though there was no towel to dry them on so she used her slacks. And the slight respite gave her time to think.

No, she didn't want to just hide out here. Maybe she could get Stan talking so she would learn, at last, what had happened to Andi.

Plus, Judge Treena's Identity Division Transformation Unit team had taught her the rudiments of self-defense—not that she was ever supposed to need to use them with her new, innocent identity.

She thought about them now, how to attack Stan—despite his gun. Beat him to the ground, then run.

Where? Could she steal his car keys first? Otherwise, how would she ever survive in the outdoors here, far from any kind of civilization?

Oh, Andi, she thought. *If you had to buy a cabin to run to for safety—why someplace like this*? She'd been in real estate. Had loved attractive homes. Weren't there any other somewhat remote locations that were just a *little* closer to civilization?

But this place gave Kelly an even better idea of how stressed, how scared, her sister had been. If only they'd talked more about it.

Fled together back then, with Eli…

But now what was Kelly going to do?

Well, she couldn't accomplish anything by staying in here for the rest of the day. She opened the door and walked out.

And didn't see Stan. Had he just left her here? Would she be that lucky?

Although if he had, how would she survive? What would she eat?

How would she return back down the hill? And—

"Okay, finished?" Stan had just reentered the one-room place through the exterior door.

"Tell me about Andi now." Kelly kept her tone calm yet insistent. No use showing even a hint of the fear she felt. "Is she hiding out here?"

She'd be shocked if Stan suggested that Andi might still be alive. Instead, the miserable SOB just laughed, his round face contorting into something macabre.

Kelly had an urge to slug him but stayed still, waiting for him to speak.

"Oh, yes, she's hiding. She didn't want to see you again at the end, you know? That's what she said when I told her I'd bring you to see this wonderful place."

Kelly felt tears rise to her eyes at the same time her fury increased a thousandfold. "So you did kill her here?" She tried to make her tone matter-of-fact instead of accusatory, no matter what she felt inside. She'd probably get more of an admission out of him that way.

As if it would do her any good now. She had no way of recording his confession. And although she would be able to testify directly now about what he said instead of trying to get the hearsay of what she'd heard from Paul Tirths into evidence, her chances of surviving this were slim to none.

But for Andi's sake, and especially Eli's, she had to try.

"Well, yes, she did die here," Stan admitted, the wryness of his smile now appearing extremely fake. "And I did kill her, but it was all self-defense. She attacked me because I was in the way of her real estate deal for that tree-hugging agency, the National Ecological Research Administration. I just figured that Jerome Baranka's property was a better fit for NERA."

"So he'd get the commission, but you'd get a lot more out of him and his political connections—and money—if he was the successful real estate seller." Kelly didn't make that a question. He could deny it if he wanted, but she knew it had to be true.

Stan just shrugged. "Come on outside while it's still light. I'll show you where your dear, interfering sister ended up."

Kelly wasn't sure where Stan had hidden his gun before, but it was back out now, pointed at her.

This was going to be it, she was sure. Yes, she might see where poor Andi had ended up—but then she would end up there, too.

Would it help if she kept Stan talking? She figured it wouldn't hurt, at least.

"So you followed Andi up here to convince her your deal was the way to go?" Kelly asked conversationally as Stan shoved her back through the door and outside onto the leaf-covered dirt surrounding the cabin.

"Sort of. The damned bitch was about to ask Regina Joralli for an appointment to speak in front of city council about the transaction and what I was going to get out of it. I figured our dear council president might be pleased to hear Andi's lies, since I'd been maneuvering to take over her position, so I got mad at Andi. She threatened to run away that night with Eli, but she'd already bought this place and I knew about it, thanks to Jerome and his knowledge of local real estate. She wasn't going to steal my son from me, so instead I threw her in my trunk and brought her here, exactly where she was headed. And when I let her out of the trunk, she ran at me, so I had to shoot her to save myself."

The man was clearly insane. Otherwise, how could he sound so calm as he spouted such horrible details of her sister's last moments? Unfortunately, that might give him *some* defense against being found guilty if he ever went to trial—which was unlikely now, of course.

They were now at the back of the cabin, and Stan led her to an area where some wildflowers were growing in a patch of yellow and red. Were they primrose and yellow pincushions? Kelly had seen some pictures of local flora online, but she wasn't sure.

What she did feel sure of suddenly was that, whatever they were, these flowers marked a grave.

"You buried Andi there?" As hard as she tried, Kelly couldn't keep the venom from her tone.

"Well, sure. Isn't it pretty?"

"It's disgusting. How could you do that to your wife? The mother of your son?"

"She deserved it," he said offhandedly, then raised the gun as if preparing to shoot Kelly.

She didn't want to die, especially not if this demon of a man would get away with killing both Andi and her.

How should she play this?

"Okay, Stan," she said. "I understand, at least kind of. But now—well, you promised Eli you wouldn't kill his aunt if he turned over that tablet to Paul. Shouldn't you check to see what's going on there?"

"I tried while you were in the john. Not that it really would have mattered. But Paul didn't answer his phone. I'm not sure what kind of mess I'm going to have to clean up when I get down the hill again, but I need to get back soon and find out. So—" He looked as if he was taking aim.

"Stan, wait. What if I take Eli, and we both move far away from you? I promise we won't say anything about our suspicions anymore, and that's all they are— suspicions. I couldn't prove anything about you then, and I can't now either." It was a lie, of course, assuming she could figure out where this cabin was again once she'd left it.

But Stan could also be lying, as usual. Maybe Andi wasn't buried there after all.

"Wouldn't you like to not have your son around making allegations against you, showing up with bruises when you hit him to keep him quiet? I can fix that. You can just say that his missing aunt showed up someplace back east, and Eli's visiting her."

He seemed to contemplate that, at least for a minute— a minute in which Kelly again surreptitiously studied their surroundings. There were tons of trees that could serve as cover, yes, but if she ran could she get far enough to hide?

Probably not.

So instead, she made herself walk closer to the flower patch, which also meant getting closer to Stan. She knelt to try to appear unthreatening.

"I don't think—" Stan began, which was when Kelly rose quickly, hurtling herself at him, aiming her shoulder toward him first, then turned away slightly in case he was able to shoot.

"You bitch!" he exclaimed as she succeeded in knocking him over, his gun hand wavering.

Kelly's mind spun through all the self-defense techniques she had learned. What was going to work for her now?

Stan lay on the ground, waving his gun in her direction. Before he got off a shot, she kicked his arm, but he didn't drop it.

She kicked again, aiming for his groin, but he had anticipated that and turned over.

She moved away slightly, attempting to figure out her next move. But this time he managed to trip her, and she wound up beside him on the ground, screaming as he grabbed at her throat and aimed the gun at her.

"Drop it, Grodon!" yelled a very familiar, very welcome male voice.

He'd done it somehow. Her hero, Alan, had learned where she was and come to save her.

Only—she was somehow thrust by Stan in front of him as he stood, his arm around her throat, the gun pressed into her side.

"Well, well. Mr. Correy, isn't it?" Stan said. "Now you'd better be the one to drop it, or I'll shoot my sister-in-law right here. You two have something going, don't you? Well, you can watch her die right in front of your eyes."

Alan froze. He had stepped out from behind a tree and was aiming his own firearm at Stan Grodon, but there was no way he could get a shot in him without harming Kelly.

He'd take a bullet himself if it would save her—but it wouldn't. The guy had an inflated ego that probably told him that his political status put him above the law he was supposed to follow and protect.

"Now, Mr. Grodon, we need to figure out a good solution here." Alan forced himself to sound calm despite the situation—and the fear and pleading on Kelly's face. "I got here first, but there are policemen on their way from Blue Haven, actual officers of the law, not just private security like me. If they see our situation, they'll arrest all of us."

"Let them," Stan spat. "You two are nobodies, interlopers who've come to my town. They'll arrest you, sure, but they'll let me go."

Alan could see the fury now in Kelly's eyes, but she had the sense to stay quiet and not tell the bastard the truth: that his days of killing, and his days in government, too, were over.

But at the moment, they were truly in a standoff. How could he save Kelly? That was the most important thing.

"Look, Mr. Grodon," Alan finally said, attempting to sound respectful. "We have a stalemate here, and someone is probably going to get hurt. Here's my suggestion. Let's all back off from one another, lay our weapons down, and you can just drive yourself back to town. I'll make sure Kelly gets back there, too. She and I will turn ourselves in at the police station, and I suggest you do the same till we get all of this straightened out."

It made little sense even to Alan, but if he could at

least convince Grodon to back down…or if nothing else, keep him talking. If he was talking, he wouldn't be shooting.

"No way!" Stan shouted. "You'll tell your lies and waste my time and—" His gun hand was moving back and forth, and he still had Kelly right in front of him. There was no way for Alan to get a clean shot in.

And if this guy was a good shot, Alan was likely to get hit, maybe die.

But suddenly, Kelly stomped on Stan's foot at the same time she grabbed his gun hand, moving downward as she dropped to the ground.

"You bitch!" Stan screamed as he attempted to regain control of his gun—but lovely, smart, brave Kelly had hold of his arm and didn't let go.

It gave Alan the opportunity he had been waiting for. He sped over, his own gun aimed at the now vulnerable Stan, and stomped on the councilman's hand till he dropped his gun.

It was over.

Chapter 23

Once a furious Stan was in the custody of the local police, Kelly threw herself into Alan's welcoming arms, right there outside the tree-shrouded cabin—and near what was apparently her sister's grave.

But before she could thank him, she had to ask about her nephew. "How's Eli?" She stepped back and stared beseechingly into Alan's compassionate brown eyes. "Did Stan force Paul to do something to him? Stan promised Eli he wouldn't hurt me as long as Andi's tablet was turned over to Paul, but I made it clear to Eli that he wasn't to do that. Especially because, even if he did turn it over, I didn't trust Paul—or Stan—not to hurt him anyway."

She watched Alan's expression morph immediately into a grin that made her melt with relief, even before his words came. "Your nephew is a hero, Kelly. I'll tell you all about it later. But he's just fine…and he's the reason I'm here."

Kelly knew her quick bark of laughter must sound hysterical. "He's the reason I'm here, too—in Blue Haven. I came to save him, but it sounds like he was the one to save me."

Alan wanted to get Kelly out of here, back down the hill and away from this place where her emotions must be strung out to the maximum.

He'd heard enough to hear Stan admit to having killed his wife Andi here, with an absurd claim of self-defense. He'd admitted burying her, too, ironically decorating her grave with attractive flowers.

He had apparently intended to do the same with Kelly.

Alan didn't want her here while that area was searched—and Andi's remains possibly dug up. But after a yelling Stan had been taken into custody, still screaming threats at the two of them, the local police had called in their crime scene investigation team, and Alan had needed to be present for that.

His job here for the ID Division was to ensure that there was adequate evidence to convict Stan Grodon for at least some of his felonies. Now Kelly/Shereen had firsthand knowledge, and she would be able to testify about what had happened here today, to her.

But kidnapping and assault were petty offenses compared with first-degree homicide, and even though Alan himself had heard some of Stan's confession, he wanted to see what evidence was uncovered related to Stan's murder of his wife.

Sure, Stan would raise his self-defense claim at trial. But given what was contained on Andi's tablet, that was likely to go nowhere.

Alan could probably have sent Kelly down the hill with some of the cops. They'd already obtained her promise to stop in at the station later so they could officially question her and get her statement.

But he didn't want to let her out of his sight.

Eventually an appropriate group from the investigation team arrived with their lighting and equipment to dig up the area, and to film and document every move.

"You don't want to be here for this," Alan said to Kelly. "Let's go into the cabin, at least."

"But you need to be here to see what they unearth. And I—as much as I don't want to view the…the remains that I think are there, I need closure, so I'll stay here, too."

It took a while since the team members had to act slowly and carefully, documenting and filming every move. It was probably the way they always conducted things. But Alan figured it was especially important to do things right when they were attempting to find evidence to ultimately convict a town leader of murder.

But it took only ten minutes or so, while he stood near the cabin holding Kelly tightly to him as they both watched the activity. Suddenly, one of the team members dressed in sanitary clothes, boots and gloves called out, "Here!" He and the others gathered around the spot he had been working at.

Kelly trembled in Alan's arms. "What did they find?" she whispered.

"We'll find out soon."

The examiners brushed dirt away as they spoke in voices that were too low for Alan to hear. But a short time later, the same guy who'd made the first discovery stood up and approached them.

His face was solemn and sympathetic as he held something out to Kelly—a necklace, with an ornate silver locket dangling from it. "Ms. Alsop," he said, for everyone had been told the basics of who she was and why Kelly—formerly Shereen Alsop—was here, "does this look familiar?"

Kelly gasped, and tears ran down her cheeks. "It looks like a necklace that belongs to my missing sister, Andi. I know I can't touch it, but can you open it?"

The man did so cautiously with his gloved hands, clearly careful not to cover over any fingerprints that might be there, although the uneven surface might be difficult to lift prints from anyway.

Kelly swallowed hard as she looked at the photos inside the locket. One was a baby picture. The other was clearly a younger Eli Grodon. "Yes, it's my sister's. Those pictures are my nephew. Then—" She bit her lips as she looked past the clearly sympathetic man. "Are there…are there remains of someone there?"

"Yes, Ms. Alsop. I'm sorry to say that there are."

They left for town shortly after that. In a way, Alan wished he didn't have to drive, since he would have liked to keep holding Kelly—he would probably always think of her as Kelly, even though she could now go by her actual name again—as she cried softly. At the moment, she sat in the passenger's seat beside him, her gaze lowered to her lap.

He didn't talk to her, not now. Trying to be cheerful might only make her feel worse, and continuing to vocalize his sympathy for what she was going through didn't sound much better.

But partway down the mountain Kelly said, "You have hands-free phone service in this car, don't you?"

"Yes," Alan said.

He saw her sit up straighter as she looked toward him as the daylight now waned. "Then let's call Judge Treena. I've wanted to talk to her before this and apologize and explain, but I didn't do it—even though I'm sure she knew just where I was and why. Right?"

"I think so," Alan agreed. He didn't want to get into what he'd done to further the judge's knowledge—nor to keep her at bay, at least at first.

"It's time, then."

"Good idea." And it was—now that things were over, and Kelly had, in fact, helped to come up with the evidence that would hopefully convict the man who had been her torturer and her sister's murderer, the reason she had needed help from the ID Division in the first place.

Alan quickly performed the technological steps necessary to call Judge Treena on his car's phone system.

"Hello, Alan." The judge's droll voice soon reverberated through the vehicle. She had obviously seen his number on her caller ID. "Have you finally gotten our subject to go back to the life we created for her?"

Alan opened his mouth to respond, but Kelly beat him to it. "That's not necessary any longer, Your Honor. I'm calling to finally apologize for running off the way I did, but also so we can tell you that we are hopefully well on our way to reaching the right conclusion of this entire situation."

For the rest of the ride, and even for a while after Alan had parked in the police department's lot, they discussed with Judge Treena what had happened.

"I still need to give my statement," Kelly finally said, looking at Alan in the glow from the light above them in the parking lot. He nodded. "Alan was kind enough to drive me to the police station, so I'd better go inside. But Judge, I can't thank you enough for all you did for me, providing me with the new identity and sending Alan here to find the evidence needed to bring my brother-in-law down."

"I'll bet you feel pretty proud of yourself that you got to help in that assignment, don't you?"

Was that amusement in Judge Treena's tone? Alan felt sure of it and smiled toward the steering wheel, instead of Kelly.

"Yes, Your Honor," Kelly said. "But I'd be really happy no matter who or what resulted in the evidence against Stan."

"We'll talk more later," the judge said. "For now, you're off the hook. But if you had just run away without this kind of conclusion, it would be a different story."

"I understand."

They ended the connection then, and Alan went inside with Kelly.

The moment she entered, she was struck full-on by a hurtling body—her nephew's. Eli was here.

"Aunt Shereen, you're all right!" He backed off just a little, smiled at her, then grabbed her close again. He looked at Alan then and said, "The police said I should come here instead of to my school. I hope that's okay."

"It's fine," Alan said.

"I'm so glad you're okay, Eli," Kelly said softly against his hair. "I want to hear all about what happened to you and how you were able to keep Paul Tirths from hurting you. Mr. Correy said you were able to lock him under the steps. And…well, we have a lot to talk about." She aimed her gaze toward Alan. It was sad, and he knew she was thinking about her sister, Eli's mom.

Eli stepped back. "I think… I think my dad is going to prison," he said unevenly. "He did some bad stuff but—"

"But, yes, he is your dad," Kelly said. "I understand how that must hurt you. One thing you can be sure of, though, is that now that you and I are together, nothing will tear us apart again. I'm going to be there for you from now on, no matter what happens to either of us."

That statement made Alan smile, even as it made him want to walk away now to give them privacy.

He had realized, when he was up on the mountain believing that Kelly/Shereen was about to be murdered, that his attraction to her was a whole lot more than what he had thought it was.

He had fallen in love with her.

Now she would be with her nephew forever. That was fine. But where would that be? What would she do now?

Alan had to return to the DC area to get his next assignment from the ID Division.

Would he ever see Kelly again?

And would she care if he didn't?

* * *

A week had passed since that horrible day when Kelly had thought Stan would murder her and torture his son with the knowledge and guilt—or worse.

She was still working at the Haven, acting as if nothing had happened—although the entire town knew about it. So did the world, it seemed. The local newspaper and TV station hadn't been the only media to get a hold of the story.

Kelly still wore her skimpy uniform—but she was glad that Stan wouldn't be around to pinch her or leer at her. She was even more glad that it appeared that justice for Andi would finally be accomplished.

But she still hadn't decided what would come next for her and Eli.

"Hey, Kelly. Or Shereen." It was one of the six customers who'd just sat down at this busy noon hour at one of her tables, a business guy in a suit. "Tell us about who you are. And what's going on with Councilman Grodon?" The man looked up at her expectantly, as did his similarly clad cohorts seated with him.

"Sorry," she said with a weak smile. "I appreciate your interest, but I have to work right now."

Which was an excellent excuse.

Nearly all the café's patrons asked for her to be their server and plied her with questions, whether or not she helped at their tables.

Still, at the moment, this job was one of the only things connecting her to reality. The Haven, and Eli.

And Alan? Oh, he had been there for her for the first couple of days after Stan's arrest, but then he'd said that Judge Treena had called him back to DC.

For his next assignment?

They'd stayed in touch by phone calls and texting, but Alan had said nothing, done nothing, to allow her to think they had any kind of a future together.

Which made her feel very sad. They had been cohorts in bringing Stan down, but their cover roles had felt very real to Kelly.

She had fallen hard for Alan—and it was just another one of the foolish things she had done, she knew. At least her coming here to help Eli had been successful.

Caring so much for Alan? Turns out it hadn't been a good idea at all.

Alan. Had thinking of him conjured him up? He had just walked through the Haven's front door, and seemed to be scanning the restaurant crowd—till his eyes lit on her. He smiled.

She couldn't help it. She smiled back as her heart leaped at seeing him here. He'd come back!

"Hey, miss," said one of the guys in a suit at her table. "Could you bring me some more coffee?"

"Of course," she said, glad for the excuse to move away through the crowded tables—but not in Alan's direction. Not yet, at least.

"I'll get it," Tobi told her, meeting up with her as she hurried to the area where the coffee service was. "I think you have something better to do." The other server's grin was knowing and suggestive. She didn't know that formerly, Kelly's supposed relationship with Alan had been an act...but then, it hadn't been one entirely.

"Thanks." Kelly handed Tobi the empty glass pot she'd been about to fill and hurried to where Alan still stood at the doorway. But she didn't get too close to him there. She couldn't have even if she'd wanted to, since Ella was with him now and they were conversing.

"Oh, thanks for joining us, Kelly," Ella said. She turned back toward Alan. "We're all aware now that's not her real name, but she's told us to keep using it since it's how we all know her."

"I get it," he said. "So, Kelly, I've just been asking Ella for some of your time this afternoon. I still have a relationship with Blue Haven Security, and therefore city council, and they're having a meeting this afternoon that they'll want refreshments served at. I hope you don't mind, but we want you to bring the food from the Haven."

Kelly felt a bit confused about the situation, but she didn't mind the request. Why had Alan come back? What did he have to do with BH Security now—and why was he still helping city council to get its refreshments?

She had an opportunity to ask him all that a short while later, after the Haven's chefs had quickly put together some sandwiches and snacks. Now Kelly and Alan carried plastic bags full of them as they walked toward Government Plaza.

"So what's really going on?" Kelly asked, keeping a short distance between them even though she'd wanted, from the moment she'd seen Alan, to throw herself into his arms and kiss him till he promised to stay around.

But that might wind up only hurting her if she tried it. She had no idea what was on his mind—or where he was living now.

"You'll get a better idea of what's up soon," he said

cryptically, and she realized that he hadn't touched her, either, let alone kissed her.

They talked about Eli on their way. Her nephew now lived with her in her small apartment. Neither of them wanted to go back to his former home. That place was still owned by Stan anyway, and even if he was convicted of all the crimes he would be charged with, Kelly didn't know what would become of his house.

Not that she wanted it. But if it could be sold and the money given to Eli, that seemed appropriate. Kelly had no hesitation about taking care of her nephew on her meager salary now. She could at least access her former bank account now that she could acknowledge, and prove, that she was Shereen. And she hoped to rent a larger apartment for them soon.

If she stayed in Blue Haven with Eli, she would try to get another teaching job, like the one she had had when she was Shereen. It would be more enjoyable to her than being a server, and it would pay better.

"So will you be staying here in Blue Haven with Eli?" Alan asked as they neared the plaza. It was as if he had heard her thoughts.

"I hope to. I want to start teaching again, as I used to do here, and he's gone through too much to add moving to somewhere unknown to the list, if I can prevent it."

"Will you be Shereen again?"

"Maybe," she said. "That's the name my teaching credentials are under. But my nickname can still be Kelly."

They had reached the bottom of the wide stone stairway leading up to the tall marble building that was the plaza. Kelly couldn't help smiling a little as she headed up the steps. She wouldn't have to worry about seeing Stan there and whether he recognized her. Not now, and never again.

It was Thursday afternoon. People were coming and going at the plaza as usual, as if nothing were different now in the makeup of the city council. And maybe nothing was officially different yet. Stan's being under arrest didn't necessarily mean he'd been kicked off the council, although surely he would be eventually. At least if he was convicted, and everything Kelly had heard recently suggested there was no question then his removal would follow.

The officials now had their evidence.

Kelly was glad about that under the circumstances, but she would have given anything, done anything, to have Andi still alive.

Once they reached the top of the steps, Alan said, "Are you still doing okay with that load?" He nodded toward the bags she held in her hands.

"I sure am." She smiled at him briefly, as if he were just a kind stranger asking about her well-being.

He hadn't acted like he was anything else since his return to her life less than an hour ago.

But when they got into the elevator to the fourth floor, Alan moved in front of the door to block anyone else from entering. Kelly, standing at the side in front of the buttons, felt a shiver of anticipation ripple through her. As if by instinct, she put the bags she held down on the floor as the door closed.

Good thing she did, since Alan's bags quickly joined them, and then she was suddenly in his arms, feeling his hard body against her, his mouth slamming down onto hers in an immediate, sensual kiss in which his lips and tongue suggested how much he had missed her.

As she had missed him.

It seemed as if they reached their floor immediately, since the door started opening again.

Kelly made herself pull away, but Alan held her there a moment longer.

"That's a good sign," he finally said against her mouth, and then he stepped back as if nothing had happened and lifted his bags again.

What was he up to?

He waited until she had also picked up her bags and exited the elevator first. Then he followed her.

"The usual meeting room?" Kelly asked, turning to look at him. Goodness, he was handsome. And his kisses...

She had to somehow keep him in her life. But how?

"Yes," he said, then led the way to the door across the hall.

Maybe this was a bad idea, Alan thought as he opened the door and stepped back for Kelly to enter first. But he wanted to wrap things up for Kelly as best as he could, let her know not only his thoughts, but how other people fit into the plans he had been working on. And fortunately, those he had asked had been amenable to helping him by being here and talking to Kelly, even though he hadn't told them his reasons for asking.

That kiss had made him hopeful that his ideas would be acceptable to Kelly. Or better than acceptable. But he couldn't be sure, and simply spouting them off hadn't seemed the best way to let her know his hopes for the future.

He followed her in. The crowd he had invited stood around near the large center table drinking coffee.

"Hey, Kelly. Glad to see you." Councilwoman Susan Arviss was the first to approach them, her hand out to relieve Kelly of one of her bags. "I've seen Eli, and he seems so much more relaxed these days. I assume it's okay with you that we're continuing the intern program here, right?"

Good. She was tacitly acknowledging that Kelly was now Eli's guardian, whether it was official yet or not. And now Kelly could discuss her nephew openly with the woman who had somewhat taken him under her wing and helped him out.

"It's great with me, Susan," Kelly said. She looked around toward the other people in the room, and then glanced back toward Alan as if puzzled.

Not surprising. They weren't all council members, although there were a few business types who had been previously entertained here now and then.

He grinned at her, then said, "Let's spread the food out on the buffet table and grab our snacks."

It was time for the fun to begin.

Less than an hour after they'd arrived, Kelly stood near the conference room door saying her farewells to those who had come and talked and asked her opinion on a lot of things.

First to leave was Dora Shallner. The part-owner and manager of the Blue View restaurant had come to express her regrets at having dated the horrible Stan

Grodon—not that she had become serious about him. But she did offer Kelly the job she had interviewed for as a server at the restaurant.

Kelly had appreciated it and hadn't outright declined, although she'd said she would keep her job at the Haven for now. Fortunately, she had already discussed staying on with Ella, who was all for it.

Kelly hadn't told Ella her hopes for resuming her teaching career, nor did she mention it to Dora now, but since it was still fall and barely into this school year, she figured she would have plenty of time to work that out for next year.

"Thanks again, Dora," she told the other woman. "I'll be in touch." It would probably be to gracefully decline the offer, but Kelly was so bemused right now that she didn't want to say anything.

Police Chief Arturo Sangler left next. He thanked Kelly for her help in gathering the murder evidence and expressed how glad he was that she hadn't been hurt. He had previously informed the group that an investigation was under way regarding Jerome Baranka and his company, and whether he had been bribing Stan Grodon to reap financial benefits from others, including the federal government. Paul Tirths also remained in custody, with charges pending against him for, at a minimum, aiding and abetting Stan. And an internal police department investigation was being conducted to make sure that the initial search into Andi's disappearance had been handled appropriately.

Council President Regina Joralli and Councilwoman Susan Arviss left together. They didn't have far to go. Regina had described in their brief meeting what would be done to kick Stan off the council and replace him. And Susan had expressed how glad she was that Eli would now have a better life, and how she hoped she and Cal would be able to get together often with Kelly and Eli.

Then there was that guy Dodd, who worked with Alan on the private security force. At Alan's request, Dodd had told the group that the head of Blue Haven Security, Nevil Hancock, had recently quit, and Alan had just been offered the job. Kelly had immediately turned toward Alan, who sat beside her. He was smiling, but there was also a question in it. Was she the reason he hadn't responded yet?

Did that mean he would actually stay here and be with her if she stuck around?

Kelly had already called Judge Treena back to discuss her hopes of staying here in Blue Haven and not returning to the life the ID Division had set up for her. Fortunately, Her Honor had figured that and said her guys were already fixing the situation. "You deserve to return to the part of your old life that works for you," the judge had concluded.

That was it. The room was empty now, except for Alan, who still stood beside Kelly.

She closed the door behind Dodd as he left, then turned to Alan.

He was immediately close at her side.

"That was a lot of information," Kelly said. "I gather you knew it all already."

He nodded. "But I thought it more appropriate for you to hear it from others before you hear what I have to say now."

The caring, questioning look in his eyes told her a lot. So did the feel of him taking her into his arms.

"We haven't known each other long, Kelly. Or Shereen. I know that. It's too early for us to promise each other forever. But what I want to hear from you is your thoughts on me accepting the job as head of BH Security and staying here and seeing how things work between us. And—"

She didn't let him finish. As she pulled his head down toward hers so she could kiss him again in response, she said, "Absolutely yes."

* * * * *